Constance C. W. Naden

The Complete Poetical Works of Constance Naden

Constance C. W. Naden

The Complete Poetical Works of Constance Naden

ISBN/EAN: 9783337378394

Printed in Europe, USA, Canada, Australia, Japan

Cover: Foto ©Andreas Hilbeck / pixelio.de

More available books at **www.hansebooks.com**

THE

COMPLETE POETICAL WORKS

OF

CONSTANCE NADEN.

WITH AN EXPLANATORY FORE-WORD BY

ROBERT LEWINS, M.D.,

Surgeon Lieut.-Colonel (Retired).

" We receive but what we give,
   And in our life alone does Nature live :
   Ours is her wedding garment, ours her shroud."
                                    —S. T. COLERIDGE.

LONDON :

BICKERS & SON, 1, LEICESTER SQUARE, W.C.

1894.

PUBLISHERS' ANNOUNCEMENT.

———

In this Complete Edition of the Poems of Constance Naden it has been deemed advisable that the two volumes, "Songs and Sonnets of Springtime" and "A Modern Apostle; The Elixir of Life; The Story of Clarice, and other Poems," should appear in the order in which they were originally published. No attempt at re-arrangement has been made. The only additions are "The Better World" (which is printed on p. 172, immediately after the conclusion of what formed Miss Naden's first volume of Poems) and three miscellaneous pieces, "Winter and Spring," "The Priest's Warning," and "Night and Morning" (which are printed last of all).

Appended to the present volume will be found a selection of Personal and Press Opinions on the Works of Constance Naden.

FOREWORD.

———•———

———

I DO not think I can submit to contemporary readers
and serious students of common-sense philosophy a
better *précis* of the principle underlying both Miss
Constance Naden's verses and prose than by repro-
duction of the following curt and concise exposition,
which adequately expresses the scope and gist both of
her Poetry and Philosophy—the former in a more or
less informal and cryptic manner, the latter in a more
formal and implicit one. The very simplicity of the
subject-matter is the principal obstacle to its acceptance.
It resolves all objects into the subject self, and thus
deals the *coup de grâce* to all Dualism whatsoever. So
that *Anima*, an ambiguous misnomer, signifying both
Life and Mind, or soul, is shown to be the product, not
the germ or source, of the Hyle or Matter—the Brain,
by its function, being the sole cause of consciousness,
without which all is blank nullity and nihility.

THE UNITY AND IDENTITY OF THOUGHT AND THING.*

Nemo potest exuere seipsum.

" Philosophy tells us that the world is a picture which we ourselves make. There is nothing in the world [including that object
itself] which we do not put there. Our whole life, then, is one
creative process."

The above affirmation of Monism and denial of dual
subject and object is taken from T. Bailey Saunders's,
M.A. (*Oxon.*), profound article on "The Origin of
Reason," in No. 160 of the *Open Court*.† It seems
completely to bear out the scientific veridity of my
title, and of Hylo-Idealism, that on the apparitional,
phenomenal, or relative theory of the universe, to which
we have alone access, Self is to Self, further than which
research is vain, the Be-all and End-all of sentient and
non-sentient existence. Hence religion is seen to have
run its baneful course, and to be superseded by reason,

* Reprinted (revised) from the *Monist*, of Chicago, for January,
1894, edited by Dr. Paul Carus, Ph.D.

† See also a lengthy and serious review of that able thinker's
" Translations from Schopenhauer" in the London *Athenæum* for
October 4th, 1890.

on which Mr. Saunders so lucidly discourses. For, if Self be all-in-all, there can be no room, in such a *pleroma*, for any *Latria* or worship, in the religious sense of the word, except Narcissus-like self-worship.

We are thus thrown back on, and face to face with, mere physical conditions, out of which *ideal* concepts proceed, while rigidly excluding all those misnamed "*spiritual*" ones, which hitherto have played so momentous a *rôle* in the destiny of humanity.* We thus make hygiene, as defined by Dr. Parkes in the solemn introduction to his manual of that last (and first) of the sciences, as not merely bodily sanitation, though that is already much, but as supreme culture of mind and body (or, to be more scientifically precise, of body merely, including brain), the all-sufficing surrogate of Divine worship. The old adage, *mens sana in corpore sano*, should thus read *corpus sanum = mens sana*, merely. This *Volte face* turns every extant ethical and mental view *topsy-turvy*. As it must do by exploding "thing" altogether, and by substituting our own thoughts for objects of all kinds. It is true, or it may be granted, that there is an objective or distal *aspect* of subjective thought. But that fact, or admission, in no degree in-

---

* It is significant and suggestive that no terms have ever been coined to express animistic concepts. Even Spirit, Soul, Lord, God, etc., are purely materialistic ones.

validates the position that the only objects cognisable are those incorporated with, and by, the subject self, from which all " things " proceed. This interpretation of the universe is, *inter alia multa*, that of the emancipated Baccalaureus in the second part of Goethe's " Faust," as enunciated in the lines thus translated by the late Constance Naden :—

> " I tell you this is Youth's [Man's] supreme vocation !
> *Before me was no world—'tis my creation :*
> 'Twas I who raised the Sun from out the sea ;
> The Moon began her changeful course with me.
> I gave the signal on that primal night
> When all the host of heaven burst forth in light.
> Who but MYSELF saves Man from the dominion
> Of dogmas cramping, crushing, Philistinian ?"

Indeed, it is the very first and last principle of common sense and common place that, before a "thing " is *perceptible*, it must be made *sensible*, and where can sensibility (consciousness) lie except in the *sensorium* which manifests that property ? On the ground alone of consciousness or sensation being a somatic office or function it can only be, like all other organic functions, an emanation of the self, and hence we are coerced into the conclusion that all things are but forms of the *Ego itself, at once both Creator and Creation.*

This non-animism thus makes each unit of humanity all that has, in pre-scientific minds where Absolutism and Dualism is the watchword of the intellect, been predicated as *Divine*. Where reason, based on positive science, comes into play, or, in other words, when man ceases to be an infant, religion or Theism disappears as a childish illusion utterly incompatible with right reason and rational ethics. All religious ideals and systems—none more than the Christian—are based on hideous immorality. For what can be more iniquitous than the doctrine of the Atonement—*i.e.*, of the vicarious sacrifice of a sinless victim for a sinful criminal? But preceding this ethical *crux* is the logical fiction. For how can the Parthenogenetic birth of Christ redeem him from the primeval "curse" entailed on all mankind by the mythical "disobedience" of our federal head and representative? From this "curse" virgins are no more exempt than their grandmothers, and thus, on its own *data*, Christianity is "hoist with its own petard." Indeed, a *replica* of Adam's abiogenetic "creation" would not serve, since earth and air partook of the "curse" entailed on our "first parents." No God is needed since man is seen to be an Autochthon, and, as such, an Anteus, who derives all the faculties required for existence out of the telluric *matrix* or *humus* (living earth) from which he sprang.

As long as the absolute doctrine of dual existence vitiated philosophy—a dual factor, in the guise of an animating principle was, or seemed, a *desideratum*. But since the inductive biological theory, which defines life as the sum of the organic functions and a physiological state, was established, man can quite rest content in the satisfactory creed that he himself—each for each— is his own law, standard, criterion, and *final* court of appeal. Clericals of all denominations are then seen to be self-evidently "kicking against the pricks," when, in our *fin de siècle* age, they attempt to bolster up the obsolete anachronism of animism (Dualism)—a quite impossible task, as I have before shown—from the incompatibility of two such factors as matter, and what they are pleased to call "spirit," re-acting on each other.

It is, I repeat, a case of pure fetichism or ghostism— the same in essence that induced the ancients to formulate their Lares and Penates, Dryads, etc., and, in short, to feign a god, or goddess, for every phenomenon from Jove, launcher of the thunderbolts, to Cloacina of the sewers !

Pope, even, in his "Essay on Man," written many years after the appearance of Newton's "Principia," could not rid himself of the notion that "ruling angels" were required to regulate the spheres. And, long after Pope, poets invoked their muse as a source of inspiration separate from themselves ! But, in our age, all such confusion of thought is a really inexcusable blunder, which must, sooner or later, prove a Nemesis to that vicious civilisation which fosters so palpable a delusion.

--

Assume, as now we *must* do, that all objects and ideas, great and small, including the abstract terms, Time, Space, and Immortality, etc., are Brain products, that Cerebration and Thought, or Mind, are one, and the seemingly paradoxical Unity and Identity for which I plead in the title of this exordium is seen to be a categoric imperative. It really is a physiological version of Kant's negation of *Thing in Itself,* from which, however, he recanted in all his works subsequent to the first edition of the "Critique of Pure Reason." It was rendered perfectly certain more than sixty years ago—a full lustre before its present opponent, Mr. Gladstone, entered public life—by Wöhler, when he artificially manufactured organic—*i.e.,* "living" out of inorganic— *i.e.,* pseudo-dead, compounds; a perfect proof that a vital Principle or *Anima,* in the sense of what is falsely interpreted as "Soul," in the religious sense of the Anglo-Saxon term for Life, is a fiction of the human imagination. An omnipotent, disposing Deity must be as much of a fetish as the Pantheon of Olympus. As is clearly seen from so many of these dispositions being failures, as lunacy, suicide, disease, premature death, and other multiform forms of Demoniac Evil. Anti-theism, therefore, not merely Atheism, as in the eighteenth century, ought to be the charter of our present state ; the Latin motto at the head of this Foreword being perfectly expugnable.

Devout nations and communities—*i.e.*, in which the public mind is addicted to religious exercises of Prayer, Praise, and Spiritualism (other-worldism) generally, are always tardigrade, and even retrograde. This rule is well exemplified in the records of the Protestant Reformation. When Luther visited Rome, saturated as he was with the diabolic and other superstitions of a Thuringian forest coal-burner, he was filled with disgust at the Atheism then prevalent amid the priesthood and cultured classes. The former openly scoffed at the Christian mysteries as *cochonerie.* He introduced into his creed, which so long has imposed on Northern Europe and New England, all these degrading *arcana.* So that, for more than two hundred years, Germany, especially, fell quite to the rear, as compared with France and England, in ethical and intellectual progress. Till the peace of Westphalia in 1648, at the close of the Thirty Years' War, all was, in that vast region, pure chaos. Indeed, till Frederic the Great's time, a century later, things were little better. Even to the very close of his reign that "first of German sons," who was himself a noted Voltairean, as Schiller pathetically laments in his fine poem, "The German Muse," cherished the opinion, which subsequent events have proved so delusive, that the Germans were "irreclaimable barbarians," as he also held Shakespeare to be, whose dramas he thought only fit for the savages of Canada. And this though in his own lifetime Kant, Schelling, Fichte, Bürger, Lessing, Herder, Goethe, Richter, and Schiller's "Robbers," which last, no doubt, was especially distasteful to the great king, were already above the horizon. David Hume, it will be remembered, delivered a similar verdict upon the English "*barbarians on the banks of the Thames.*" He held them as already quite below the pale of Philosophy—a verdict fully corroborated by Lord Bacon in his essay on "The True Greatness of Kingdoms," and on "The Wisdom of the Ancients." Commerce he especially held to flourish during the disruption and decay of nations.

R. LEWINS, M.D.,
Surgeon Lieut.-Col. (Retired).

Army and Navy Club, Pall Mall.

CONTENTS.

—

THE ASTRONOMER, Etc.

B

THE LADY DOCTOR, Etc.

SONNETS.

TRANSLATIONS *(see also p. xxii.)*.

A MODERN APOSTLE, ETC.

RESIPISCENTIA, Etc.

EVOLUTIONAL EROTICS.

SONNETS.

TRANSLATIONS *(see also p. xx.)*.

FRAGMENTS.

DEDICATION.*

To J. C. and Caroline Woodhill.

YE who received me, when your hearts were sore,
    With double welcome, since I came in lieu
    Of one whose fond embrace I never knew—
Your child, my mother, dear for evermore—
Who scarce had time to greet the babe she bore,
    But, dying in her spring, bequeathed to you,
    Her father and her mother, guardians true,
One little life, to tend when hers was o'er :

Ye who have watched me from my infant days
    With tenderest love and care, who treasure yet
Quaint sayings, sketches rude, and childish lays ;
Accept this wreath, entwined in April hours :
    Yours was the garden where the seed was set,
To you I dedicate the opening flowers.

---

* This Dedication and the Motto on the next page were originally prefixed
to Miss Naden's first volume of poems, " Songs and Sonnets of Springtime."

" Nicht länger wollen diese Lieder leben
    Als bis ihr Klang ein fühlend Herz erfreut,
Mit schönern Fantasien es umgeben,
    Zu höheren Gefühlen es geweiht ;
Zur fernen Nachwelt wollen sie nicht schweben,
    Sie tönten, sie verhallen in der Zeit,
Des Augenblickes Lust hat sie geboren
Sie fliehen fort im leichten Tanz der Horen."

SCHILLER.

THE ASTRONOMER, Etc.

c

POEMS.

THE ASTRONOMER.

WHITE, cold, and sacred is my chosen home,
    A seat for gods, a mount divine ;
And from the height of this eternal dome,
    Sky, sea, and earth are mine.

All these I love, but only heaven is near,
    Only the tranquil stars I know ;
I see the map of earth, but never hear
    Life's tumult far below.

Bright hieroglyphs I read in heaven's book ;
    But oft, with eyes too dim for these,
In half-regretful ignorance I look
    On common fields and trees.

Scant fare for wife and child the fisher gains
From yon broad belt of lucent grey;
Rude peasants till those green and golden plains;
Am I more wise than they?

Oh, far less glad! And yet, could I descend
And breathe the lowland air again,
How should I find a brother or a friend
'Mid earth-contented men?

Though, while I sat beside my household fire,
Some dear, dear hand should clasp my own,
Must I not pine with home-sick, sharp desire
For this my mountain throne?

I were impatient of the narrowed skies,
Yes, even of the clasping hand;
And she, sad gazing in my restless eyes,
Would haply understand,

And know my fevered yearning to depart,
To dwell once more alone and free:
Well might I love, yet needs must break the heart
That puts its trust in me.

Yet hope and ecstasy desert me not,
   But coldly shine, like moonlit snows ;
This earthly dream, renounced yet unforgot,
   To heavenly splendour grows.

For oft, when sleep has lulled a brain o'erwrought,
   Strange light across my brow is thrown ;
The glorious incarnation of my thought,
   Urania stands alone.

She, passionless, of no fond woman born,
   Towers awful in her virgin grace ;
Calmly she smiles ; the first faint rose of morn
   Flushes her sovereign face.

Her atmosphere of white unswerving rays
   Athwart the fading moonlight swims ;
Rare vapour, like a comet's luminous haze,
   Floats round her argent limbs.

Her clear celestial eyes look deep in mine,
   Her brow and breast gleam icy pure ;
She whispers—" Be thy heart my secret shrine,
   So shall thy strength endure.

" So shall thy god-like wisdom soar above
    All rainbow hues of grief or mirth,
And I will love thee as the stars do love
    Even thy distant earth."

Then her eyes lighten, then her voice thrills clear,
    But life and death contend in me ;
And still she speaks, but now I may not hear ;
    Shines, but I dare not see.

How shall immortal splendour wed the gaze
    Of man, who knows but that which seems,
Whose sight were blinded, if the sun should blaze
    With unrefracted beams ?

Void were the earth and formless, if arrayed
    In purity of perfect white ;
All things are clear by colour and by shade,
    Glorious with lack of light.

But what is she, whose beauty makes me blind,
    Whose voice is like the voice of Fate ?
What, save a lustrous mirage of the mind,
    My slave, whom I create ?

Yet from such dear illusions Wisdom springs,
   Though these may fade she shall not die ;
In fabled forms of heroes and of kings,
   E'en yet we map the sky.

Slow-conquering Truth loves well the joyous noon,
   But silent midnight gave her birth ;
The cone of darkness that o'ershades the moon
   Revealed the orbëd earth.

Man knelt to constellated suns supreme,
   But as he knelt to golden clods,
Nor, till he ceased to worship, e'er could dream
   The greatness of his gods.

He wove for all the planets as they passed
   Strange legends, wrought of love and youth,
While o'er the poet-soul was vaguely cast
   A shadow of the truth.

Kinsman is he to all the stars that burn
   Mirrored in eyes of sleepless awe ;
And from his brotherhood with dust, may learn
   The heavens' living law.

Nor shall the essences of Truth and Might
  Sleep ever in thick darkness furled :
You dim horizon bounds my present sight,
  Not the eternal world.

When the skies glitter, when the earth is cold,
  In some divine and voiceless hour,
The heavens vanish, and mine eyes behold
  The elemental Power.

Now has the breath of God my being thrilled ;
  Within, around, His word I hear :
For all the universe my heart is filled
  With love that casts out fear.

In one deep gaze to concentrate the whole
  Of that which was, is now, shall be,
To feel it like the thought of mine own soul,
  Such power is given to me.

My sight, love-strengthened, Time and Space con-
    trols ;
  No more are Force and Will at strife ;
Beyond the sun I pass ; around me rolls
  Infinite-circled Life.

This realm where he his destined orbit keeps,
  This world of planet-ruling spheres,
Borne onward with its Pleiad-centre, sweeps
  Through unimagined years.

In suns, that shining for some nobler race
  Their twin-born light commingled give,
And through black depths of interstellar space
  A boundless life I live.

To me the orbs their fiery past reveal,
  With each minutest change designed ;
Till, in this harmony of worlds, I feel
  The future of mankind,

When each shall aid the universal plan,
  When every deed its end shall serve,
When e'en the wildest comet-thought of man
  Shall flash in ordered curve,

When mighty souls, that burst all prison bars,
  Shall their diviner selves obey,
When man shall hold communion with the stars,
  Constant and calm as they,

When every heart shall perfect peace attain,
  And every mind celestial scope ;
Such were mine own, save for this hungry pain,
  This lack of earth-born hope.

I were content, though palsied, sightless, dumb,
  If, blasting toil-worn brain and eye,
The heights and depths of human joy to come
  Shone clear, before I die.

THE CONFESSION.

Oh, listen, for my soul can bear no more ;
   I crave not pardon ; that I cannot win :
Yet hear me, Father, for I must outpour
      My tale of deadly sin.

This night I passed through dim and loathsome lairs,
   Where dwell foul wretches, that I feared to see :
Yet would to God my lot were such as theirs !
      They have not sinned like me.

And then I saw that lovely girl who stood
   Here, where I stand, some venial fault to show :
I was as fair, as innocently good,
      One long, long year ago.

High thoughts were mine, and yearnings to endure
   Some noble grief, and conquer heaven by pain :
Alas, I was a child ; my prayers were pure,
      Yet were they all in vain.

Love came and stirred my breast ; not fierce or vile,
  But springing stainless, like some mountain stream ;
And I was happy for a little while,
      And lived as in a dream.

Thou art a priest, and dwellest far apart ;
  In vain I speak of joys thou hast not known :
Even to *him* I scarce could show my heart,
      Although it was his own.

Nay, look not in my face !   One night he came,
  And I sprang forward, giddy with delight :
Father !   His blood-stained hands !   His eyes aflame !
      His features deadly white !

Ah, wherefore ask me more ?   Some hated foe—
  But 'tis a common tale—thou knowest all :
A word, a gesture ; then a sudden blow ;
      And then—a dead man's fall.

Dumbly I heard, and could not weep or sigh ;
  Gone was all power of motion, e'en of breath ;
But from my heart rose up one silent cry,
      My first wild prayer for death.

"Farewell," he said, "farewell!   Yet bury deep
My bloody secret, that it shall not rise ;
Or it will track and slay me, though I sleep
Nameless, 'neath foreign skies."

Such boon he craved of me, his promised wife :
Earth's hope, heaven's joy, for him I lost the whole :
Some give but love, and some have given life,
But *I* gave up my soul.

"Embrace me not," I said.   But ere he went
One long impassioned kiss he gave me yet :
Still, still we loved—oh, Father, I repent—
Would God I could forget !

Ah, not to fiery love would Christ deny
The gift of mercy that I cannot seek :
Father, a guiltless man was doomed to die,
And yet I did not speak.

Mine was the sin ; for me it was he died,
Slain for the murder that my Love had wrought :
How blest was he, when Death's gate opened wide,
And Heaven appeared unsought !

But I, who dared not seek the Virgin's shrine,
　　Whose very faith was madness and despair,
Lived lonely, exiled far from Love Divine,
　　　　From peace, from hope, from prayer.

None dreamt that I consumed with secret fire,
　　Nor knew the sin that withered up my youth :
I wasted with a passionate desire
　　　　Only to tell the truth.

But now they say that he I love is dead ;
　　Calmly I listen ; see, my cheeks are dry ;
My heart is palsied, all my tears are shed ;
　　　　And yet I would not die.

Let me do penances to save his soul,
　　And pray thy God to lay the guilt on me ;
Strong is my spirit ; I can bear the whole,
　　　　If that will set him free.

For could my expiating woe and shame
　　Raise him to Paradise, with Christ to dwell,
Then were there joy in purgatorial flame—
　　　　Nay, there were Heaven in Hell.

And then, perchance, when countless years are past,
   Ages of torment in some fiery sea,
The grace of God may reach to me at last ;
     Yes, even unto me.

THE ROMAN PHILOSOPHER TO CHRISTIAN PRIESTS.

WELL have ye spoken, but the words ye said
   Stir in my constant soul nor love, nor rage;
Through you my life is bare, my joy is dead,
   Yet speak I calmly, as a Roman sage.

Behold the myriad orbs, whose light from far
   Darts through the spherëd heavens, when day is
      done:
What if the dwellers in yon faintest star
   Deem its weak light more glorious than the sun?

And were it granted those dim eyes to share
   The glow of noon that glads our earth and sea,
Would they not hate the white unpitying glare,
   And choose to dream in starlight, e'en as ye?

Clear truth to vulgar minds no comfort yields ;
　The fair old myths have served their purpose well :
Is Heaven more bright than our Elysian fields ?
And was not Tartarus sufficient Hell ?

Till now, the ancient symbols have sufficed ;
　But there is room for all ; the world is wide :
Zeno was great, and so, perchance, was Christ,
　And so were Plato, and a score beside.

If I were young, I might adore with you ;
　But knowledge calms the heart, and clears the eye :
A thousand faiths there are, but none is true,
　And I am weary, and shall shortly die.

It is not rest, to stand for evermore
　And chant with myriads round a flaming throne ;
I crave not this your heaven ; my life is o'er,
　And I would slumber, silent and alone.

Ye cannot give me back my one desire :
　How have ye changed my daughter, my delight !
Since I, forsooth, must writhe in quenchless fire,
　While she sings anthems, clad in vestal white !

I have not warred with doctrines, but with deeds ;
   In fair and generous mood I met you first ;
I hated not her teachers, nor their creeds,
   And yet she scorns me as a thing accursed.

She deems my lordly house unclean, defiled ;
   She scarce will sip my wine, or taste my bread.
Ye boast of virgin martyrs—if my child
   Die for her faith, my vengeance on your head !

Ye sons of slaves, unworthy to be free !
   Calmly I speak, yet fear me, crafty priests !
I will arouse the people—they shall see
   Your bodies hacked with knives, or torn by beasts.

Go, eat and drink, and call your feast divine ;
   But, if my daughter dies, ye shall not live :
The ancient Roman spirit still is mine,
   And I forget not, neither can forgive.

THE LAST DRUID.

DESPAIRING and alone,
Where mountain winds make moan,
   My days are spent :
Each sacred wood and cave
Is a forgotten grave
   Where none lament.

This is my native sod,
But to a stranger God
   My people pray ;
Till to myself I seem
A scarce remembered dream
   When morn is gray.

I know not what I seek ;
My heart is cold and weak,
   My eyes are dim :

Across the vale I hear
An anthem glad and clear,
  The Christians' hymn.

Oh, Christ, to whom they sing,
Thou art not yet the King
  Of this wild spot ;
I am too weary now
At new-made shrines to bow ;
  I know Thee not.

They say, when death is o'er
Man lives for evermore
  In heaven or hell ;
They call Thee Love and Light :
Alas ! they may be right,
  I cannot tell.

But if in truth Thou live,
If to mankind Thou give
  Life, motion, breath ;
If Love and Light Thou be,
No longer torture me,
  But grant me death.

Give me not heaven, but rest ;
In earth's all-sheltering breast
   Hide me from scorn :
The gods I served are slain ;
My life is lived in vain ;
   Why was I born ?

Gone is the ancient race ;
Earth has not any place
   For such as I :
Nothing is true but grief ;
I have outlived belief,
   Then let me die.

These dim, deserted skies
To aged heart and eyes
   No comfort give :
Woe to my hoary head !
Woe ! for the gods are dead,
   And yet I live.

THE CARMELITE NUN.

SILENCE is mine, and everlasting peace ;
My heart is empty, waiting for its Lord ;
All hope, all passion, all desire shall cease,
And loss of self shall be my last reward.

For I would lose my life, my thought, my will ;
The love and hate, the grief and joy of earth :
I watch and pray, and am for ever still ;
So shall I find the death, which yet is birth.

Yet once I loved to hear the wild birds sing,
I knew the hedge-row blossoms all by name ;
Keen sight was mine, to trace the budding spring,
Clear voice, for songs of joy when summer came.

Too dear I held each earthly sight and sound,
Too well I loved each fair created thing,
And when I prayed to Him I had not found,
I called Him in my heart "the mountains' King."

All, all is past—gone, every vain delight ;
   No beauty tempts me in this lonely cell :
Yet why, O Lord, were earth and sky so bright,
   Winning the soul that in Thyself should dwell ?

Often my heart recalls the sacred time
   When fell the tresses of my nut-brown hair ;
But then will come—O God, forgive the crime !—
   That guilty question—Can I still be fair ?

I cannot quite forget that I am young ;
   I sometimes long to see my mother's face :
Oh, when I left her, how she wept, and clung
   About my neck in agonized embrace !

And there was one—Ah, no, the thought is sin—
   Why come these thronging forms of earthly grace ?
Close, close, my heart !   Thou shalt not let them in,
   To break the stillness of this holy place.

Oh, Mary, Mother, help me to endure !
   I am a woman, with a heart like thine :
But no—thy nature is too high and pure,
   Thou canst not feel these low-born pangs of mine.

Oh, for the vision of the Master's face !
Oh, for the music of the heavenly throng !
I have but lived on earth a little space,
And yet I cry, " How long, O Lord, how long?"

THE ALCHEMIST.

In lonely toil my manhood has been spent,
    Spurning all ties of home, all joyance free ;
And now my heart is sick, my frame is bent,
    And I would sleep, but rest is not for me.

Two gifts I seek, two wondrous powers unknown
    Shall yield their treasures to my dauntless mind ;
The meaner, boundless wealth to me alone ;
    The nobler, endless life for all mankind.

My star of distant hope doth far transcend
    All dew-drop glories, that around me lie :
With Nature I will struggle to the end ;
    Conquer I must, though conquering I should die.

Though I should die, ere I have tasted life,
    Losing the heritage I give to all ;
Though, as I grasp the trophy of the strife,
    My battle-wearied arm should powerless fall.

I conquer still, though strength may not be mine
   To drink the cup my dying hand prepares ;
My life, but not my triumph I resign,
   For all mankind shall be my deathless heirs.

I care not who the victor's crown may wear,
   I care not, though my bones neglected lie :
This is my latest, this my only prayer—
   Come life, come death, let not my wisdom die.

Yet oh ! sweet Life, for whom I long have served,
   Whose glorious beauty I from far have seen,
Not this reward thy votary deserved,
   Not this thy warrior's guerdon should have been.

Oh no, it cannot be ! for I shall live,
   And priceless bounty royally impart,
And life and love, and wealth and gladness give,
   Dug from the treasure caverns of my heart.

I still will hope, and struggle for the crown ;
   Night shall not come, before I grasp the truth ;
For I will yet behold my just renown,
   And feel at last the fresh delight of youth.

THE SCULPTOR.

BEFORE the noblest form his genius wrought
   The sculptor stood : with awe, but not with pride,
He saw the image of his highest thought,
   His inner self, transfigured, purified.

He spoke with sad emotion, half concealed,
   Like one who sorrows, but would fain rejoice ;
No glad content was in his eye revealed,
   Nor any thought of triumph in his voice.

" This is my grand ideal. 'Twas for this
   I gave my strength, while yet an eager boy ;
Leaving fresh mirth for some diviner bliss,
   Trusting to Hope my fair estate of joy.

" But hope is gone for ever. I am left
   With this sublime fulfilment of my dreams ;
Not of the midnight loveliness bereft,
   Yet clear and steadfast in the noonday beams.

"Oh, that some charm were wanting ! that some stain
   Marred the ideal grace that my vision wore !
For I may live, but cannot hope again,
   And I may toil, but shall advance no more.

" I saw my rival frown, his cheek turn pale,
   In envy of the fame so dearly bought ;
But this I know—the hope of those who fail
   Is better than the victory they sought.

" Yet in my heart some new delights may spring,
   As humble flowers on lordly ruins live ;
Still shall my work some tranquil pleasures bring,
   Though not the ecstasy it once could give.

" I do not grieve that glowing youth is spent,
   Nor would I quench the yet remaining fire ;
Since lofty joy dwells not with calm content,
   Nor peaceful happiness with strong desire."

THE SISTER OF MERCY.

SPEAK not of passion, for my heart is tired,
I should but grieve thee with unheeding ears ;
Speak not of hope, nor flash thy soul inspired
In haggard eyes, that do but shine with tears.
Think not I weep because my task is o'er ;
This is but weakness—I must rest to-day :
Nay, let me bid farewell and go my way,
Then shall I soon be patient as before.
Yes, thou art grateful, that I nursed thee well ;
This is not love, for love comes swift and free :
Yet might I long with one so kind to dwell,
Cared for as in thy need I cared for thee :
And sometimes when at night beside thy bed
I sat and held thy hand, or bathed thy head,
And heard the wild delirious words, and knew
Even by these, how brave thou wert, and true,
Almost I loved—but many valiant men
These hands have tended, and shall tend again ;
And now thou art not fevered or distressed

I hold thee nothing dearer than the rest.
Nay, tell me not thy strong young heart will break
If to thy prayer such cold response I make ;
It will not break—hearts cannot break, I know,
Or this weak heart had broken long ago.
Ah no ! I would not love thee, if I could ;
And when I cry, in some rebellious mood,
" To live for others is to live alone ;
Oh, for a love that is not gratitude,
Oh, for a little joy that is my own !"
Then shall I think of thee, and shall be strong,
Knowing thee noblest, best, yet undesired :
Ah, for what other, by what passion fired,
Could I desert my life-work, loved so long ?
I marvel grief like thine can move me still,
Who have seen death, and worse than death, ere now—
Nay, look not glad, rise up ; thou shalt not bow
Thy knee, as if these tears thy hope fulfil :
Farewell !   I am not bound by any vow ;
This is the voice of mine own steadfast will.

THE WIFE'S SONG.

I. NIGHT.

SHE kneels with folded hands, as though she prayed ;
  Over her pure, pale cheek the moonlight streams,
And o'er the slender form, in white arrayed ;
  Her room is consecrate to bridal dreams,
And she is like some lonely priestess-maid,
  Believing, though her god be silent long,
  And in his temple chanting secret song.

"'To heaven I lift my longing eyes,
  Knowing that yonder tranquil moon
Is bright for you in western skies.
  And has she power your soul to tune
In subtlest harmony divine
With all the passioned thoughts of mine ?

" Nay, rather let her give you rest,
  In peace to sleep, with joy to wake ;

Yet, if a dream the slumber break,
Dream of my yearning lips and breast,
Hungered and lone, far off and sad,
But dream them near, and dream them glad !"

II. MORNING.

Now has she slept ; nor fell there any blight
   Over her beauty from those wakeful hours ;
Her darkest grief was but a moonlit night,
   Tuneful with birds, and sweet with summer flowers,
Closed by an early daybreak of delight ;
   And now she lifts anew her matin chant,
   With all the garden choir conjubilant.

" The morning sunshine floods my room,
   Its tender glow my brow has kissed,
And scattered all the night-born gloom ;
   Yon, floating, thin, translucent mist,
Pierced through and through with living gold
   Makes lovelier what it half enshrouds,
And you in distant skies behold
   The self-same sun, but other clouds.

" Trim English lowlands bloom for me,
    For you, Atlantic waves are bright ;
For both, o'er earth, and sky, and sea,
Through thought and passion, mind and heart,
    Still streams the same all-glorious light :
Earth's barriers keep us far apart,
    But we are one at heaven's height."

A LETTER.

Only a woman's letter, brown with age,
    Yet breathing deathless love, too strong and deep
E'er to be told, save by the written page,
    That cannot blush, or hesitate, or weep :
Only a letter, treasured by the dead ;
    Voiceful, yet ever powerless to impart
    Its hidden melodies to any heart
Alien from hers who wrote, from his who read ;
Save as a lute long silent, waked at last
    By heedless fingers, or by winds that thrill
    The chords untuned, may feebly murmur still
Some love-sweet echoes from the tuneful past.

Take my one treasure : take, and ever keep
    My whole heart's love : nor shall the gift be vain,
    Although it cannot bring you rest from pain,
Nor glad forgetfulness, nor tranquil sleep.

Oh, that my power were boundless as my love !
   Then would I give to him I hold so dear
   Joys faintly dreamt by many an ancient seer,
Chanting sweet fables of the heavens above.

"Alas," I thought, "such dreams are all too bright,
Too poor am I, of god-like gifts to sing ;"
   But you have said that even these I bring ;
You tell me, that to raptured touch and sight,
   I seem the essence of ethereal Spring,
The incarnation of perfume and light.
Wherefore I will not grieve, but gladly twine
   Amid your mellow fruit my virgin flowers :
   All have their time for love, and this is ours :
Let us rejoice, while yet the sun doth shine.

THE MYSTIC'S PRAYER.

My God, who art the God of loneliness,
   Who, Life of human souls, art yet alone,
Who, Lord of joy, dost bear the world's distress,
   Come Thou, and quench my being in Thine own ;
   Come, in this mute cathedral make Thy throne
While moonlight through the blazoned window streams,
   Where kings and saints a ceaseless vigil keep ;
Their reflex glories, like celestial dreams,
   Haunt the grey carven brows of those who sleep,
   Illuming changeless eyes, that will not wake and
      weep.

Thy sleep, O Christ, hath sanctified their calm ;
   Their hands point upward ; yet nor wish nor care
Doth move Thy tranquil souls to join the psalm
   Sung in this ancient home of tears and prayer.
Yes, these are dead ; but I, who live and breathe,
Would learn of them, and dying would bequeath

A memory of one, who deaf to sound
Communed with Silence, guardian of all truth ;
  Who, with divinest midnight compassed round,
  The secret soul of earth and heaven found,
And knew the heart of death, wherein are life and
    youth.

For this one hope I wrestle, day and night ;
  In this one faith I joined thy chosen saints,
And left my virgin love, my young delight,
An earth-born cloud, that seemed most fair and white
  Until I looked beyond, and saw the sun,
And blinded by his beams, desired not sight.
  Now might I dream that heaven is almost won,
Save that yon pale Madonna's plaintive smile
  Thrills me with anguish, till my spirit faints,
Till, even in this lone cathedral aisle,
  A sad voice murmurs—" Didst thou scorn thy life
For love of God ? and hath He sealed thy choice ?
  A maid contented, or a happy wife
I might have been."   Hush, Lord, this bitter voice.
  I am not worthy, save of Thy disdain,
Yet unto Thee have I performed my vow,
  And tortured soul and sense, and prayed for pain ;
It cannot be that Thou wilt scorn me now,
  That thou hast let me toil and agonize in vain.

Not martyrdom I crave, nor length of days ;
But grant me, Lord, ere this frail form decays,
  The perfect union that my soul has sought,
The ecstasy that knows nor prayer nor praise,
  The raptured silence, unprofaned by thought.
No more wilt Thou in heavenly dreams appear,
  When of Thy mystic Essence I am part,
For mine own soul I see not, nor can hear
  Even the pulsings of this fevered heart,
Fevered and weary ; but full calm is near ;
Almighty calm, in endless being blest,
Infinitude of life, too deep for aught save rest.

THE PILGRIM.

THERE was a land, where all men lived in dreams,
   Where heaven was hid by vapours, grey or gold ;
Yet real seemed their life, as our life seems,
   And lovers wooed, and merchants bought and sold ;
But e'en 'mid feast, and song, and soft caress,
Each heart was sore with utter weariness.

And some were rich, some miserably poor,
   And each for other felt a dull contempt ;
And some were fools, of loftiest wisdom sure,
   And some seemed wise, but no man knew he dreamt ;
If any woke, men shrank with angry fear,
Or smiling said, " What doth this dreamer here ?"

But at the last, one minstrel boy awoke,
   And strove to rouse his fellows, but in vain ;

Till, strong and flushed with hope, away he broke,
    And left them revelling in mirthful pain :
His hands were trembling from a last embrace,
Yet somewhat sternly smiled the youthful face.

His golden singing-robes were cast aside,
    The roses all were shed, that wreathed his brow ;
No more 'mid guilty dreams might he abide,
    Who in his heart had sworn a solemn vow
To find the ancient innocence again
In some far land unknown of weary men.

No kindred nature deemed his purpose good ;
    The vision and the promise were his own :
High hills he climbed ; through many a tangled wood
    He cut his way, in darkness and alone,
Or built a trembling bridge where wild waves tossed,
    Or in a fragile boat the surges crossed.

On sandy plains he saw fair miraged lakes,
    And oft he hungered, and was oft athirst ;
Through haunts of savage beasts and venomed snakes
    He roamed, still bravest when the path was worst ;

Toiling for heedless kinsfolk unforgot,
For those delirious hearts, that knew him not.

But when he next shall speak, they *must* awake ;
   Or if this last best triumph may not be,
Yet will he struggle, e'en for life's dear sake—
   What lustre blinds him ?   Has he strength to see
That primal Heaven on Earth, desired so long,
Won with no joy-burst, greeted with no song ?

Oh, glorious recompense for vanished youth,
   For love untasted, for the silenced lyre !
This is indeed that ancient land of truth,
   Nobler than thought, more lovely than desire :
The snow-crowned heights are girt with blossoms sweet,
And grass lies cool beneath his fevered feet.

But is there respite here for soul and flesh ?
   Are yonder glades but homes of idle calm ?
This is no dreamland—here the wind blows fresh,
   Lulling the sense with no voluptuous balm ;
Full life inspires the pilgrim's heart and eyes
From yon bright waves, yon high unclouded skies.

Shall he not twine fresh garlands for his head,
   And seek new singing-robes of quaint device?
Here roses blush, more delicately red
   Than e'er he dreamed the flowers of Paradise,
And in this lovely land is plenteous store
Of gems and gold, more rich than once he wore.

Ah no !   Exulting 'neath yon radiant sky
   For youth's forgotten songs he oft may yearn ;
But the unflinching hand, the wakeful eye,
   Still tireless to their lonely task shall turn :
Ere his limbs fail, ere his strong heart be dumb,
Let him make plain the path, that all may come.

THE PANTHEIST'S SONG OF

IMMORTALITY.

BRING snow-white lilies, pallid heart-flushed roses,
   Enwreathe her brow with heavy-scented flowers ;
In soft undreaming sleep her head reposes,
   While, unregretted, pass the sunlit hours.

Few sorrows did she know—and all are over ;
   A thousand joys—but they are all forgot :
Her life was one fair dream of friend and lover ;
   And were they false—ah, well, she knows it not.

Look in her face, and lose thy dread of dying ;
   Weep not, that rest will come, that toil will cease :
Is it not well, to lie as she is lying,
   In utter silence, and in perfect peace ?

Canst thou repine that sentient days are numbered ?
   Death is unconscious Life, that waits for birth :
So didst thou live, while yet thy embryo slumbered,
   Senseless, unbreathing, e'en as heaven and earth.

Then shrink no more from Death, though Life be
    gladness,
  Nor seek him, restless in thy lonely pain :
The law of joy ordains each hour of sadness,
    And firm or frail, thou canst not live in vain.

What though thy name by no sad lips be spoken,
    And no fond heart shall keep thy memory green ?
Thou yet shalt leave thine own enduring token,
    For earth is not as though thou ne'er hadst been.

See yon broad current, hasting to the ocean,
    Its ripples glorious in the western red :
Each wavelet passes, trackless ; yet its motion
    Has changed for evermore the river bed.

Ah, wherefore weep, although the form and fashion
    Of what thou seemest, fades like sunset flame ?
The uncreated Source of toil and passion,
    Through everlasting change abides the same.

Yes, thou shalt die : but these almighty forces,
    That meet to form thee, live for evermore :
They hold the suns in their eternal courses,
    And shape the tiny sand-grains on the shore.

Be calmly glad, thine own true kindred seeing
   In fire and storm, in flowers with dew impearled ;
Rejoice in thine imperishable being,
   One with the Essence of the boundless world.

LIGHT AT EVENTIDE.

Evil has brought forth good, but good in turn
Brings evil forth, and painfully we learn
    The rich resulting harmony of life :
Triumphant glories, that most brightly burn,
      Last not the longest ; for the worth of strife
Consists not in the crown the victors earn.

The man who truly strives can never fail ;
    For though at set of sun
    The battle is not won,
    And he is left, despairing and alone ;
Yet through the gloom, when flesh and spirit quail,
    New radiance flashes, e'en to hope unknown.

He that can walk in darkness, will not slip
    Although some bright surprise
    At first may blind his eyes ;
The ancient glow comes back to heart and lip,
    And tears remembered make his laughter wise.

Fresh love and joy, not seeking, he shall find,
    While Truth at last her promised garland weaves,
Not of gay roses or green laurels twined,
    But bright with scarlet berries, amber leaves.

In some fair glade he seems awhile to rest,
    All Dead Sea fruits forgot ;
Wild songsters chant, wild breezes blow :
His path is overgrown, his brow caressed
    By blossoms, that he did not sow,
      And foliage, that he tended not.

And what though once, in vain yet noble quest,
    With burning feet and eyeballs dim,
He strove to scale volcanic heights of power ?
    Since on the fertile terrace grew for him
Wisdom and Love, rich fruit and glorious flower.

BOOKS.

Oh, fatal fruits, nurtured with tears and blood!
To taste your richness, we have given youth,
Unshadowed mirth, and calm credulity;
Your heavy perfume spoils the wild-flower scent
Wafted around us by the winds of heaven.
Ye steal the young delight, that was so sweet,
The simple, thoughtless joy in all things fair,
Giving instead a weary questioning,
A striving for what cannot be attained,
A cloudy vision of the inner life.
We might have lingered in our paradise,
Hearing no music sadder than the notes
Of dreamy birds; while Hope and Memory,
Still young and fair and gaily innocent,
Still undefiled by any touch of doubt,
Together trod the dewy meads of life.

Thus said I, in unreasoning complaint,
Bitterly railing on the friends I love

Because their voice and sweet companionship
Must bring the grief that ever comes with joy.
My heart was full : each common sight and sound
Seemed fraught with mournful meaning ; and the earth
Was like a hopeless bride, bedecked in vain
With gems and flowers, for one who will not come.
What wonder I rebelled against the art
That taught me thus to think in metaphors,
And gave me reasons for my soul's unrest ?
For I remembered not that it had drawn
My higher nature forth, and given voice
To secret melody.   I missed the truth
That knowledge is a greater thing than mirth.
And aspiration more than happiness.

F

MEMORY.

PRECIOUS glimpses through the future's curtain
    He may catch, who sees the past unveiled ;
Else, in seeking for a goal uncertain,
    Blindly groping, will and heart had failed.

What were love, its faded flowers uncherished ?
    What were life, its bygone days forgot ?
Memory may live, when hope has perished ;
    Hope were dead, if we remembered not.

All our past, in colours soft and tender,
    Stretches backward, till it melts in night ;
While the future, robed in hazy splendour,
    Shows us transient phantoms of delight ;

Glorified reflections of the present ;
    Spirits of the days that once have been ;
Hopes of bright perfection, when life's crescent
    Fills the orbèd outline, dimly seen.

Yesterday's delights will haunt to-morrow,
  Subtle essences of vanished joys,
Till the spectre of remembered sorrow
  Their ethereal witchery destroys.

Rays of memory have sunned our pleasure ;
  In the self-same light regret will spring ;
Sorrow is man's burden, yet his treasure ;
  Proves him servant, yet proclaims him king.

Sharpest anguish, meaner things besetting,
  Finds a perfect and a swift relief :
Man alone, immortal, unforgetting
  Wears the sombre coronal of grief.

In his heart a quenchless fire is burning,
  Kindled ere his conscious life began :
Lord of restless thought and noble yearning
  Reigns in loneliness the soul of man.

Yet the earth must yield him free communion,
  Heights of heaven his daring hope must gain,
Till he joy in that eternal union
  Which the struggling spirit may attain.

Linking Past, and Present, and Hereafter
  Man shall find a staff, where seems a rod :
Solemn memories, that check his laughter,
  Draw him nearer to the heart of God.

LIGHT-BORN SORROWS.

HATH Wisdom made thee weep? Be yet more wise,
And sing for joy. The blind man, gaining sight,
Says haply, "Would I ne'er had seen the light!
This world is all so strange, my 'wildered eyes
Know nought of fair or foul : ah, dear content,
Ere any spectre came to me at night,
When, watched and soothed by unimagined skies,
My dreams were nought but music and sweet scent.
Now must I link to faithful touch and tone
A wondrous alien form, unloved, unknown,
And try to read the face that may be sweet
When I have learnt its language—not till then.
E'en if I shut my eyes, am blind again,
And strive, undoubting, that dear voice to greet,
To trust the hand, that still must guide my feet,
The phantom that I know not comes between ;
I must look up—I, who was blind from birth,
And conning wistfully her face and mien,

Interpret mystic features by clear voice,
Loving the song, must love the plumage too,
And make the rose's scent explain its hue :
Thus, keeping faith in beauty, I rejoice,
(Or hope for joy) in green fields, heavens blue,
In all my new-found plenty, felt as dearth,
In all enigmas of this visible earth."

Ah, think ye not, if that poor man be wise,
He will exult because his night is past,
Saying " Although it come to baffled eyes,
Yet light is good, and shall be sweet at last :
From this new face, that even now grows dear,
I shall but learn more richly cadenced love,
And all this foreign world, around, above,
Shall float like music to my inward ear ;
Amid all discords, through all thunder-strife,
My soul shall glory in perfected life."

ON THE MALVERN HILLS.

In pleasant shade I walk, while sunshine lies
    On many a distant slope,
And far above me, gold-green summits rise,
    Like steadfast towers of Hope.

My hands are full of wreathëd bryony,
    And bracken from the hill ;
And sated with the beauty that I see
    My very heart is still.

Lonely I step o'er this elastic sod ;
    All living things are dumb ;
But whispering of heights I have not trod
    The mountain breezes come.

Only a little while my heart can rest,
    A little while forget
The rugged paths to many a sun-lit crest
    That must be mounted yet.

Take, wild fresh winds, my fading flowers and fern ;
   These joys I may not keep :
Sweet slumberous glade, farewell !   When I return,
   It will be time for sleep.

JANUARY 28TH, 1880.

No more I long for April's fitful sheen,
    For little fluttering lives, that passed in June,
       For leaves and flowers, by sad October lost ;
Since now in ecstasy mine eyes have seen
    The rich blue heaven of a summer noon
       O'er dazzling trees, thick-robed with mossy frost.

Amid the leafless hedge-rows jewel-twined,
    Great trunks and boughs, not crystal-clad as they,
       Like black majestic arches I behold ;
All wreathed and crowned with woven sprays, defined
    In every tender shade of pearly grey,
       And radiant white, that glitters into gold.

Around the mighty limbs all gnarled and bowed,
    The oak-tree twigs are finely interlaced ;
       The willows droop in bright cascades of foam,
Each distant tree, a white and feathery cloud,
    The nearer branches, delicately traced,
       And gleaming pure against the azure dome.

The winds are hushed—there comes no murmuring
     breeze
  To stir the poplar's lofty sun-lit cone,
    Or myriad branchlets of the wide-spread beech :
Through this all-glorious temple of the trees,
    As through the house of God, I walk alone ;
     A silence, as of worship, is their speech.

SPRINGTIDE.

The silver birch, with pure-green flickering leaves,
Flooded by morn with golden light, rejoices,
And mingles with the kindred merriment
Of perfume-laden winds and happy voices :
No child of spring is lonely, but receives
Some subtle charm, by diverse beauty lent,
And with another life its own inweaves ;
E'en man's creative eyes win all their gain
From light, whose glory, but for him, were vain.
While bud the flowers, while May-tide sunshine beams,
Through all the world of mind and body streams
One constant rapture of melodious thought,
One fragrant joy, with summer promise fraught,
And one eternal love illumes the whole ;
For odour, light, and sound are truthful dreams,
Inspired by Nature in the human soul.
This fresh young life, whereof my own is part,
With boundless hope all earth and heaven fills ;

The birds are waking music in my heart,
A voiceless chant, more sweet than they can sing ;
My thoughts are sunbeams ; all my being thrills
With that exultant joy whose name is Spring.

NOONDAY.

The deep enchantment of the summer-tide
    Lay o'er the earth, and hill and valley dreamed,
And all the trees with light were glorified,
    That through the half-transparent foliage gleamed.

The sunbeams brightly pierced the deep-red beech,
    Kindling the sombre leaves to scarlet flame :
Like half-articulate, melodious speech,
    The thousand murmurs of the noonday came.

All sounds were mingled in one dreamy tune ;
    All joys were fused in one supreme delight :
No hope, no fear, profaned that lustrous noon,
    Nor any dim forebodings of the night.

It was a poet's paradise of rest,
    Where, for a season, heart and brain might sleep :
Not now by passion and by thought possessed,
    Yet ripening golden grain, that they must reap.

Grain to be harvested with anxious toil,
  Winnowed and crushed, till fullest worth be won :
But first, in light and heat, the fruitful soil
  Receives the inspiration of the sun.

And even night, with depth of mystic gloom,
  And even Autumn, with its slow decay,
Bring no more solemn message than the bloom
  And joyful splendour of a summer day.

To each grand thought, some beauteous form replies ;
  The soul, exalted to its noblest height,
Grows, like the pure, illimitable skies,
  The chosen home of Mystery and Light.

TWILIGHT.

THE radiant colours in the west are paling ;
  Fast fades the gold, and green, and crimson light,
And softly comes, each trivial object veiling,
  The all-ennobling mystery of night.

This is the hour of thought and silent musing,
  When poets' fancies tender buds unfold ;
Like the sweet primrose of the twilight, choosing
  To spend on evening noonday's gift of gold.

These blossoms hide within their deep recesses
  Treasures the wandering wind can never seize ;
Not all its inner wealth the flower confesses,
  Nor gives its choicest perfume to the breeze.

What wizard's wand can charm the secret sweetness
  From the fair prison, where it lies concealed ?
What poet's lay can show in grand completeness
  The inmost heart, by human speech revealed ?

We twine the spell of rich harmonious numbers,
    We conjure up the graceful words in vain :
Our lighter fancies waken from their slumbers ;
    Without a voice the noblest thoughts remain.

So dash the restless billows of the ocean,
    But bring no tidings of the tranquil deep ;
Above, are endless tumult and commotion ;
    Below, are silence and eternal sleep.

Beneath the realms that human skill discloses,
    Where Life and Death have ceased their ancient
        fight,
The deep foundation of the earth reposes,
    A temple sacred to primæval night.

In wild rejoicing, and in vengeful madness,
    Men haste o'er vale and mountain, sea and shore,
But calmly, underneath their grief and gladness,
    The earth's great secret lies for evermore.

Above, the sky with myriad stars is gleaming ;
    Fair in their light the sleeping land appears ;
And yet that radiance, o'er the earth down-streaming,
    Tells not the wonders of the distant spheres.

And far beyond the realms of starlight glory
   Are mysteries too high for Fancy's wing,
Nameless alike in science and in story
   In all that sage can tell or poet sing.

As height and depth alike transcends our vision,
   The human soul whence clearest lustre beams,
Has yet its Hades and its fields Elysian,
   Revealed alone in symbols and in dreams.

For there are griefs, that none has ever spoken,
   Joys, that no mortal tongue has power to tell ;
The silence of the soul must be unbroken
   Till to the speech of earth we bid farewell.

YEARNING.

I MURMUR songs of past delight,
    To tunes of present pain :
Around me is the empty night
    That answers not again.

My thoughts were better told by tears,
    And yet I scorn to weep :
Forgetting hopes, forgetting fears,
    My eyes and heart shall sleep.

Yet must I see, in visions wild,
    The joys I cannot gain,
And, like a little lonely child,
    Stretch out my arms in vain.

CHANGED.

THEY told me she was still the same,
  In form, and mind, and heart ;
With freshly-dawning joy I came,
  And now in grief depart.

Still round the forehead, smooth and white,
  The golden tresses twine,
The face is fair, the step is light,
  As when I called her mine.

And yet the mouth that once I kissed
  Is not the same as then ;
The smile of love I never missed
  Comes not for me again.

More measured is the silver voice,
  The words more fitly said ;
But while she speaks, I half rejoice
  To feel my love is dead.

The eyes are deeper than before,
    And far more subtly sweet ;
And yet I pray that mine no more
    Their altered glance may meet.

My dream is past.   I loved a child,
    The woman I resign ;
The world and she are reconciled,
    And now she is not mine.

SIR LANCELOT'S BRIDE.

Soft blows the breeze, the sun shines bright,
 The birds sing loud and gay ;
But from the castle on the height
 Sounds forth a blither lay.

The hall is decked with flowerets fair,
 The gates are opened wide,
To welcome home that youthful pair,
 Sir Lancelot and his bride.

The lingering hours pass slowly by,
 The blossoms droop and fade ;
And many a bright impatient eye
 Looks down the rocky glade.

" Look forth, my son, adown the height,"
 Outspeaks a harper old ;
" Methought I saw a helmet bright
 Flash back the sunset's gold."

"Sir Lancelot's band draw nigh, my sire,
    Their hundred helmets gleam,
And like a line of living fire
    They ford the shallow stream.

" Hurrah ! hurrah ! they come, they come !
    But why so slow and sad ?
Why march they not to beat of drum,
    With shouts and laughter glad ?

" Oh, sweet and sad their music streams,
    In cadence low and long ;
More like a funeral dirge it seems
    Than a gay bridal song."

" Look forth again," the old man said,
    " Thy sight is strong and clear ;
What bear they on that narrow bed,
    That looks so like a bier ?"

" I see the gleam of golden hair,
    As slowly on they ride :
For weird in beauty, strangely fair,
    They bring Sir Lancelot's bride.

" They bear her through the rocky dale ;
   Methinks they sigh and weep :
My lady's cheek is deadly pale—
   Oh, say, can that be *sleep ?*

" She lies in all her loveliness,
   A fair yet awful sight ;
And that is not her bridal dress,
   That gleams so ghastly white.

" The light falls on her lily cheek,
   And on her golden head—
Oh, hush, or but in whispers speak :
   Say not—that she is dead !

" Alas, alas ! in deep despair
   Sir Lancelot's head is bowed :
He hides his face ; he cannot bear
   To see the snow-white shroud."

Within the hall the flowerets fair
   Ere now have drooped and died ;
Fit welcome to that mournful pair,
   Sir Lancelot and his bride.

The morn shall come with brighter flowers,
   The lark shall warble gay ;
But never more shall Lancelot's towers
   Send forth a gladsome lay.

THE ABBOT

SLOWLY, with dream-like sadness, tolled
    The monastery bell ;
The Abbot of those cloisters old
    Lay dead within his cell.

The monks were gathered round his bed ;
    Solemn and still they stood ;
The fearful presence of the dead
    Awed that stern brotherhood.

They gazed upon his hoary head,
    And on his noble brow ;
They saw the form whence life had fled—
    Where was the *spirit* now ?

Strong will was his, a nature stern,
    That loved nor wine nor gold :
Did youthful passion ever burn
    Within that bosom cold ?

The monks had loosed his rugged vest,
    While yet alive he lay :
What saw they on that wasted breast
    That gleamed so golden gay ?

No shining cross, no image fair,
    Those eager brethren found ;
Only a tress of golden hair,
    With a black ribbon bound.

They gazed upon that witness dumb,
    That told of love and death ;
Some spake with scorn, with pity some,
    But all with bated breath.

" Lay it again upon his breast,"
    An ancient brother said ;
" His soul hath entered into rest ;
    Judge not the silent dead.

" Long hath he lived a life apart
    From every earthly snare ;
Yet who shall say what aching heart
    Throbbed 'neath his shirt of hair ?

" Blame not his long-enduring love,
   Nor call it weak and vain,
But pray that he, in realms above,
   May meet his bride again."

They buried him beneath the shade
   Of cloisters grey and old ;
And near his silent heart they laid
   That treasured lock of gold.

DAS IDEAL.

"Denn sehet, das Reich Gottes ist inwendig in euch."

Luc. xvii. 21.

Meinem verehrten Freunde Herrn Dr. Lewins in
Dankbarkeit gewidmet.

Ich bin ein Sonnenkind, und strebe immer
    Hinauf zum ew'gen Licht;
Der Erdentag, der enge Wolkenschimmer
    Stillt meine Sehnsucht nicht.

Genügt es mir, auf Bergeshöh' zu wohnen,
    Der scheuen Gemse gleich?
Nein! wo kein Adler schwebte, muss ich thronen,
    Wie in der Ahnherrn Reich.

Zerreissen will ich die geträumten Schleier
    Des Stoffs, des Raums, der Zeit,
Und mich ergiessen, frei und immer freier,
    In die Unendlichkeit.

Nie soll es mir an Brüdergeistern fehlen,
  Wie hier im Lügenrauch ;
Das todte Weltall will ich selbst beseelen,
  Mit leichtem Gotteshauch.

Der Wind verstärkt sich nur durch eignes Wehen,
  Die That gebiert die Kraft :
Ich *bin* noch nicht.   Erst kann der Mensch entstehen,
  Wenn er als Gott erschafft.

Umsonst ! Was hilft's, dass sich der Wahrheit Funkeln
  Zu vollem Tag vermehrt ?
Selbst auf dem Sonnenthron muss sich verdunkeln
  Das Herz, das stets begehrt.

Wie sollt' ich laben mein verdurstet Wesen
  Mit leerem, schwankem Schein ?
Nur an der Erde Brust kann ich genesen
  Von scharfer Himmelspein.

Verzeih' mir, o Natur, das kind'sche Lallen,
  Den rasenden Gesang :
Doch was bist *Du*, als nur das Wiederhallen
  Vom alten Seelenklang ?

Der kühne Dichtertraum ist nicht verloren,
　Er war zu eng, zu bleich :
Nur in des Menschen Seele wird geboren
　Das Erd- und Himmelreich.

THE LADY DOCTOR, Etc.

THE LADY DOCTOR.

Saw ye that spinster gaunt and grey,
Whose aspect stern might well dismay
   A bombardier stout-hearted?
The golden hair, the blooming face,
And all a maiden's tender grace
   Long, long from her have parted.

A Doctor she—her sole delight
To order draughts as black as night,
   Powders, and pills, and lotions;
Her very glance might cast a spell
Transmuting Sherry and Moselle
   To chill and acrid potions.

Yet if some rash presumptuous man
Her early life should dare to scan,
   Strange things he might discover;
For in the bloom of sweet seventeen
She wandered through the meadows green
   To meet a boyish lover.

                     H

She did not give him Jesuit's bark,
To brighten up his vital spark,
   Nor ipecacuanha,
Nor chlorodyne, nor camomile,
But blushing looks, and many a smile,
   And kisses sweet as manna.

But ah ! the maiden's heart grew cold,
Perhaps she thought the youth too bold,
   Perhaps his views had shocked her ;
In anger, scorn, caprice, or pride,
She left her old companion's side
   To be a Lady Doctor.

She threw away the faded flowers,
Gathered amid the woodland bowers,
   Her lover's parting token :
If suffering bodies we relieve,
What need for wounded souls to grieve ?
   Why mourn, though hearts be broken ?

She cared not, though with frequent moan
He wandered through the woods alone
   Dreaming of past affection :

She valued at the lowest price
Men neither patients for advice
   Nor subjects for dissection.

She studied hard for her degree ;
At length the coveted M.D.
   Was to her name appended ;
Joy to that Doctor, young and fair,
With rosy cheeks and golden hair,
   Learning with beauty blended.

Diseases man can scarce endure
A lady's glance may quickly cure,
   E'en though the pains be chronic ;
Where'er that maiden bright was seen
Her eye surpassed the best quinine,
   Her smile became a tonic.

But soon, too soon, the hand of care
Sprinkled with snow her golden hair,
   Her face grew worn and jaded ;
Forgotten was each maiden wile,
She scarce remembered how to smile,
   Her roses all were faded.

And now, she looks so grim and stern,
We wonder any heart could burn
   For one so uninviting;
No gentle sympathy she shows,
She seems a man in woman's clothes,
   All female graces slighting.

Yet blame her not, for she has known
The woe of living all alone,
   In friendless, dreary sadness;
She longs for what she once disdained,
And sighs to think she might have gained
   A home of love and gladness.

MORAL.

Fair maid, if thine unfettered heart
Yearn for some busy, toilsome part,
   Let that engross thee only;
But oh! if bound by love's light chain,
Leave not thy fond and faithful swain
   Disconsolate and lonely.

THE OLD LOVE-LETTERS.

To-day I've discovered a treasure
  Tied up with a ribbon of blue ;
That record of pain and of pleasure,
  A packet of old billets-doux.

The note-paper, quite out of fashion,
  The date of ten summers ago,
Recall the unreasoning passion
  Of juvenile rapture and woe.

No face was so lovely as Minnie's,
  I praised it in prose and in verse ;
Her curls were like piles of new guineas—
  Alas, she had none in her purse !

I loved her for beauty and kindness,
  I grieved when I fancied her cold,
But Cupid, quite cured of his blindness,
  Now takes a good aim at the *gold*.

To fair Lady Flora, the heiress,
    I've offered my love and my life ;
Repenting of ancient vagaries,
    I'll settle to wealth and a wife.

The heat of my boyhood is banished
    Alike from my heart and my head ;
The comet for ever has vanished,
    But fireworks will answer instead.

I've kept all my ardent effusions,
    Appeal, protestation, and vow :
I'm cured of my youthful delusions,
    And can't write such love-letters now.

The thing was excessively silly,
    But then we were only eighteen,
And she was all rose-bud and lily,
    And I was uncommonly green.

I'm happy to say she was fickle,
    She blighted my love with a frown ;
It withered, ere Time with his sickle
    Could cut the first blossoming down.

We parted—how well I remember
  That gloomy yet fortunate day !
It seemed like the ghost of December,
  Aroused by the frolics of May.

I shook myself loose from her fetters—
  (I did not express it so *then*) ;
'Twas well she returned me the letters,
  For now I can use them again.

I am not afraid of detection,
  I cast all my scruples away ;
The embers of former affection
  Shall kindle the fire of to-day.

LOVE *VERSUS* LEARNING.

Alas, for the blight of my fancies !
 Alas, for the fall of my pride !
I planned, in my girlish romances,
 To be a philosopher's bride.

I pictured him learned and witty,
 The sage and the lover combined,
Not scorning to say I was pretty,
 Nor only adoring my *mind*.

No elderly, spectacled Mentor,
 But one who would worship and woo ;
Perhaps I might take an inventor,
 Or even a poet would do.

And tender and gay and well-favoured,
 My fate overtook me at last :
I saw, and I heard, and I wavered,
 I smiled, and my freedom was past.

He promised to love me for ever,
    He pleaded, and what could I say ?
I thought he must surely be clever,
    For he is an Oxford M.A.

But now, I begin to discover
    My visions are fatally marred ;
Perfection itself as a lover,
    He's neither a sage nor a bard.

He's mastered the usual knowledge,
    And says it's a terrible bore ;
He formed his opinions at college,
    Then why should he think any more ?

My logic he sets at defiance,
    Declares that my Latin's no use,
And when I begin to talk Science
    He calls me a dear little goose.

He says that my lips are too rosy
    To speak in a language that's dead,
And all that is dismal and prosy
    Should fly from so sunny a head.

He scoffs at each grave occupation,
   Turns everything off with a pun ;
And says that his sole calculation
   Is how to make two into one.

He says Mathematics may vary,
   Geometry cease to be true,
But scorning the slightest vagary
   He still will continue to woo.

He says that the sun may stop action,
   But he will not swerve from his course ;
For love is his law of attraction,
   A smile his centripetal force.

His levity's truly terrific,
   And often I think we must part,
But compliments so scientific
   Recapture my fluttering heart.

Yet sometimes 'tis very confusing,
   This conflict of love and of lore—
But hark ! I must cease from my musing,
   For that is his knock at the door !

MOONLIGHT AND GAS.

THE poet in theory worships the moon,
    But how can he linger, to gaze on her light?
With proof-sheets and copy the table is strewn,
    A poem lies there, to be finished to-night.
He silently watches the queen of the sky,
    But orbs more prosaic must dawn for him soon—
The gas must be lighted ; he turns with a sigh,
    Lets down his venetians and shuts out the moon.

"This is but a symbol," he sadly exclaims,
    "Heaven's glory must yield to the lustre of earth ;
More golden, less distant, less pure are the flames
    That shine for the world over sorrow and mirth.
When Wisdom sublime sheds her beams o'er the night,
    I turn with a sigh from the coveted boon,
And choosing instead a more practical light
    Let down my venetians and shut out the moon."

He sits to his desk and he mutters " Alas,
  My muse will not waken, and yet I must write !"
But great is Diana : venetians and gas
  Have not been sufficient to banish her quite.
She peeps through the blinds and is bright as before,
  He smiles and he blesses the hint opportune,
And feels he can still, when his labour is o'er,
  Draw up his venetians and welcome the moon.

THE TWO ARTISTS.

" EDITH is fair," the painter said,
   " Her cheek so richly glows,
My palette ne'er could match the red
   Of that pure damask rose.

" Perchance, the evening rain-drops light,
   Soft sprinkling from above,
Have caught the sunset's colour bright,
   And borne it to my love.

" In distant regions I must seek
   For tints before unknown,
Ere I can paint the brilliant cheek
   That blooms for me alone."

All this his little sister heard,
   Who frolicked by his side ;
To check such theories absurd,
   That gay young sprite replied :

"Oh, I can tell you where to get
    That pretty crimson bloom,
For in a bottle it is set
    In Cousin Edith's room.

"I'm sure that I could find the place,
    If you want some to keep ;
I watched her put it on her face—
    She didn't see me peep !

"So nicely she laid on the pink,
    As well as *you* could do,
And really, I almost think
    She is an artist, too."

The maddened painter tore his hair,
    And vowed he ne'er would wed,
And never since, to maiden fair,
    A tender word has said.

Bright ruby cheeks, and skin of pearl,
    He knows a shower may spoil,
And when he wants a blooming girl
    Paints one himself in oil.

MAIDEN MEDITATION.

" I'll don my kerchief blue," she said,
  " And wear my Sunday gown,
For every morn, with lightsome tread
  A youth goes by to town.

" And ever as he passes by,
  Methinks he walks more slow,
And glances up, with wistful eye,
  To where I sit and sew.

" And sometimes, with a tender sound
  He whistles soft and low ;
How can that gentle youth have found
  That I love music so ?

" His flashing eyes reveal his soul,
  They are so very bright ;
And ever in his button-hole
  He sticks a lily white.

" He never dons a flaunting rose,
    But always wears the same ;
Perhaps it is because he knows
    That Lily is *my* name !

" I'll wear a wreath of lilies white
    Methinks, when I'm a bride—
Oh, here he comes, with footstep light--
    But—who walks at his side ?

" It's some one in a scarlet shawl ;
    Perhaps *he* calls her fair,
But *I* don't think she's nice at all :
    I hate that yellow hair !

" How *can* he walk with such a fright ?
    Oh dear, what *shall* I do ?
He's given her that blossom white !
    Is *her* name Lily too ?

" But now I look at him, he seems
    Less handsome than before ;
His eyes have lost their radiant gleams,
    His voice is sweet no more.

" His hair, methinks, is getting red,
　　His nose less straight appears :
I could not such a creature wed,
　　Though he should sue for years !

" And other youths for me may sigh,
　　And I may love again,
But never, never more will I
　　Watch at the window-pane !"

LAMENT OF THE CORK-CELL.*

FAREWELL, oh mocking Wind!   No more I mix
    Thine airy substance with my world, the Tree :
Farewell, oh Carbon, that I cannot fix,
    And Oxygen, that I no more set free !

They tell me I have helped the trunk to grow,
    The roots to suck the earth, the boughs to fork,
The fruits to ripen—well, it may be so,
    But I am dying, and shall soon be cork.

Dead, sapless cork ! yet I remember still
    My moist and merry life in windy March ;
How green I was ! how full of chlorophyll !
    But soon it shrivelled, leaving only starch.

---

* Towards the end of summer, the cells immediately beneath
the epidermis of a young shoot usually become converted into
cork.   Their green colour is changed to brown, and the walls are
rendered almost impervious to water, so that vital functions are no
longer possible.

Blest epoch ! when transparent and elastic,   .
   My membrane scarce restrained its endoplast,
When, homogeneous, semi-fluid, plastic,
   My vital molecules rotated fast.

Dry as I am, I once was young and tender,
   Alive with chemic yearnings ; then, alas !
What thoughtless joy was mine, in spring tide splen-
      dour,
   To decompose carbonic acid gas !

Oh, had I sunk to inorganic slumber,
   And left the atoms to their gaseous glee !
The greatest pleasure of the greatest number
   My life may serve—but what is that to me ?

Backward I look, as o'er a fearful chasm,
   To days when I rejoiced to live and grow ;
Now less and less becomes my protoplasm,
   My nucleus divided long ago.

My wall grows thicker, dryer—oh to issue
   From this dark prison, where compressed I dwell,
To live, no more a part of any tissue,
   But a primordial protoplasmic cell !

A cell amœboid, drifting from its mother,
   Naked and houseless in the cruel storm,
Having no aid of sister or of brother,
   Nor any cellulose to keep it warm ;

Yet having freedom !   Nay, the dream I banish,
   The time of cell-division long is past ;
Slowly and surely, all my contents vanish,
   My walls are waterproof—I'm cork at last !

SIX YEARS OLD.

THEY'VE left me alone in the garden,
    So I'll talk to that dear little wren—
Mr. Beetle! I *do* beg your pardon,
    I was very near killing you, then.

I'll tell you a tale, Mrs. Robin,
    Please do not be frightened at all—
A tale about Neddy and Dobbin—
    She's gone! she's flown over the wall!

That wall must be *very* old—maybe
    They're the children of Israel's bricks;
It was built before I was a baby,
    And now—only think—I am six!

Six years old! What a beautiful swallow,
    Catching flies! How I wish he could speak!
He's gone down to that house in the hollow;
    I went there to dinner last week.

I could stay in that garden for ever,
    And make friends with the beeches and limes :
I saw Dr. Jones—he's *so* clever ;
    He writes to the papers sometimes !

He looked at me hard through his glasses,
    And said, " Now make plenty of noise,
Have a regular romp with my lasses,
    And be petted and teased by the boys."

He said that my curls wanted rumpling,
    My cheeks should be red and not pink,
He called me a sweet little dumpling—
    He's very insulting, I think.

'Twas Nurse that had made me so tidy,
    And how can I help being small ?
He gave me some roses on Friday ;
    Perhaps he is nice, after all.

I stayed with the children till seven ;
    They're kind, but so dreadfully rough !
There were ten of them—I made eleven—
    We played Tick, French and English, and Buff.

The girls are as bad as their brothers,
   They teased me, and played me such tricks !
But Maude isn't rude like the others,
   She says I look older than six.

She showed me her dog and her kittens,
   And the birds, and the fish in the pool :
She crochets her scarves and her mittens,
   And goes to Miss Trimmington's school.

She mustn't make blunders or stammer,
   Or stoop when she sits on the bench ;
She knows History, Science, and Grammar,
   Geography, Tables, and French.

She takes pepper and mustard at dinner,
   She may ask for plum-pudding again :
I wish I were taller and thinner,
   I wish—how I *wish*—I were ten !

She has brothers and sisters—a dozen—
   And Rover, and Pussy, and Poll ;
But I haven't even a cousin,
   I've only Mamma, and my doll.

Papa's out all day in the City,
    And I'm often in bed when he comes :
He's so tired and so grave—what a pity !
    When *will* he have finished his sums ?

I wish there were more of us, only
    It's nice to play just what I please ;
And when I am mopish and lonely
    I always can talk to the trees.

Mamma says, " Sweet flowers will not tarry,
    But trees are companions for life."
I wish that great lime-tree could marry,
    With me for his dear little wife !

Sometimes, when I shoot at the sparrows
    (I don't want to hit them, they know),
I peel his small twigs for my arrows,
    And bend a strong branch for my bow.

If he died, oh, how much I should miss him !
    (It's only his *dry* sticks I peel)
I put my arms round him and kiss him,
    And sometimes I think he can feel.

Those beautiful green caterpillars
    Live here, that Nurse cannot endure ;
And the birds—cruel butterfly-killers !
    But they don't know it's wrong, I am sure.

I make tales about flying and creeping,
    About branches, and berries, and flowers ;
And at night, when I ought to be sleeping,
    I wake and lie thinking for hours.

I keep quiet, that Nurse may not scold me,
    And think, while the stars twinkle bright,
Of the tales that Aunt Mary has told me,
    And wonder—who comes here at night ?

I fancy the fairies make merry,
    With thorns for their knives and their forks ;
They have currants for bottles of sherry,
    And the little brown heads are the corks.

A leaf makes the tent they sit under,
    Their ball-room's a white lily-cup :
Shall I know all about them, I wonder,
    For certain, when I am grown up ?

Far over the seas and the mountains
　There's a wonderful country of light ;
My new home—full of castles and fountains :
　My Dolly goes there every night.

I've seen it in dreams—there are plenty
　Of birds and beasts, talking in verse ;
I shall take Mamma there when I'm twenty,
　And Papa, and Aunt Mary, and Nurse.

Papa will look glad, when I show him
　Such new and such beautiful things ;
He'll be pleased when I write my grand poem,
　And paint a bright angel with wings.

I'll swim, with a mermaid and merman,
　Through the seas and the ocean so broad ;
I'll learn French, and Italian, and German,
　And soon be as clever as Maude.

I'll often have tea at Aunt Mary's,
　With marmalade—orange and quince :
I'll visit the queen of the fairies,
　And then I will marry a prince.

SONNETS.

JANUARY, 1879.

WITH bounding heart, with eyes and cheeks aglow,
   Not caring how the frost may stab and sting,
   I haste along, where leafless branches fling
Their clear blue shadows o'er the sun-lit snow.
For though I count sad Winter as my foe,
   Within my heart I can create the Spring,
   Can hear sweet music, ere the thrushes sing,
And see white flowers, before the pear-buds blow.

These homely scenes, whence first my childish eye
   Its own ideal form of beauty chose,
I love for ever ; leaves and blossoms die,
But this ethereal image lingers yet ;
   And if I grieved, I could but grieve for those
Who know not spring, or having known, forget.

TO A HYACINTH IN JANUARY.

SWEET household hyacinth, whose dainty breath
   Steals through my spirit like an April dream !
   Each day I watch another snowy gleam,
That dawns and brightens through thine emerald
     sheath :
The encircling air, the water from beneath,
   The fireside glow, the pallid noon-day beam,
   Arise transfigured in thy white raceme,
Safe from the New Year's wind, whose touch were
     death.

The bells of Spring are not so sweet and fair,
   For they with wind and rain and hail must cope,
   That all too soon their tender life destroy ;
But thou, warm sheltered from the frosty air,
   Art like some delicate and hidden hope,
     More full and fragrant than the promised joy.

TO THE FIRST SNOWDROP.

Fair, sunny-hearted child of many tears !
  Thou, while thy mother Earth forsaken slept,
  Didst gather to thyself pure hopes, that crept
Through stormy dreams ; and now the sun appears,
White buds reflect each rare faint smile, that cheers
  The home where thine unshapen germ was kept,
  Safe in deep midnight, while the heavens wept,
Or hung the shuddering trees with frosty spears.

Now springs to life and light each buried joy,
  With broken music and with tearful glow,
With drooping blossoms, winter-pale and coy ;
For Love shall soon fulfil her long desire—
  Her face and breast are memories of snow,
Her heart, like thine, is lit with vestal fire.

MARCH, 1878.

The blackbird sits and pipes his love-notes clear
   In yon dark tracery of budding sprays,
   Sharply defined against the distant haze,
But soon 'mid fresh green leaves to disappear :
Now soft, now keen, the wind breathes hope and fear,
   While with unsheltered almond flowers it plays :
   The skies are sad, remembering winter days,
But birds and blossoms know that Spring is here.

I, too, foresee her glory, and rejoice ;
   Though to my heart she comes in wintry guise,
Dark-robed, slow-stepping ; for in eye and voice
Are promises of music and of light,
   And I can wait till smiles shall come for sighs,
And golden hues for grey, and bloom for blight.

MARCH, 1879.

Ye little birds, that chant your love so loud,
 Your careless hearts are not so glad as mine,
 For he who sings because the sun doth shine
Is robbed of joy by every murky cloud ;
And ye, sweet heralds of the summer crowd
 Of unremembered flowers, whose tints combine
 To light the meadows—ye grow pale and pine,
When by cold winds your radiant heads are bowed.

From you, from all fair creatures of the earth,
 I do but gain the beauty that I give ;
Your form, your music, in my soul have birth,
 And in my very life your colours live ;
 And when the sunlight fades, and ye depart,
 I hold your joy within my secret heart.

K

CLEAR, golden, soft, the spring-tide sunshine beams,
　　With tranquil splendour piercing grove and
　　　　dingle,
　　As though bright morning, noon, and eve could
　　　　mingle
In some eternal home of daylight dreams ;
　　Even as though this radiance were not fleeting,
　　　But shone for ever from the slumbering skies,
　　　Calming with tender light impassioned eyes,
　　And sleepless brain, and heart too strongly beating.

Yet cold March winds prepared these breezes warm,
　　And heralded this glow of April weather,
　　And soon dim flakes of cloud will float together,
Till earth be sad once more with rain and storm :
　　For all fresh glory must be born of strife,
　　And still perfection were but death in life.

MAY, 1879.

At last, coy Spring, concede one festal day
   To us who yearn thy beauty to behold ;
   These pallid leaves, that peer above the mould,
Perfume and brighten ; lanes and woods array
With hawthorn, that was wont to bloom in May,
    White-petalled, crimson-anthered ; lilies cold,
    With drooping bells that hide their central gold,
And sun-bright buttercups and cowslips gay.

Long have we listened to a song of death,
   That wild winds chant o'er living seeds en-
      tombed :
Sing thou of life ; inspire us with thy breath ;
  Transfuse thy lustre e'en through clouds and
     showers ;
   Our hearts shall glow, like dells by thee illumed,
Whose shadows are but images of flowers.

THE grey old church is solemn in the sheen
    Of noonday—half its reverend beauty won
    From that blind, silent, lifeless denizen
Who sleeps within ; whose living soul is seen
In tall and arching lindens, freshly green,
    With light leaves golden-twinkling in the sun :
    In all sweet May-tide joyance, new begun,
That sings or blooms where frost and snow have been :
    And in the rippling, daisy-bordered river,
That flashes back the joy of God and man,
    And whispers to fresh hearts, that wake and
        quiver,
Such melodies, as round young Shakespeare wove
    Their spells, while near his feet the Avon ran,
Changeful, yet changeless, e'en as life and love.

IN THE LANES BETWEEN STRATFORD AND SHOTTERY, MAY 14TH, 1880.

THROUGH dreamful meads, that still his spirit keep,
    Roamed the boy-poet, when the morn was young,
    And listened while the skylark's mirth out-rung,
Though his own heart was warbling strains more
    deep ;
And 'mid half-wakened king-cups, thought of sleep
    More sweet than theirs, that waited till he sung,
    And bade it flee ; then to his eyes there sprung
Such gladsome tears, as waking, she might weep.

Here with his Love he wandered to and fro,
    Yet 'mid his utmost passion of desire,
High hopes, deep thoughts, had room to live and
    grow ;
Here, while he mused of old heroic strife,
    His blood leapt through his veins, a fount of fire,
And all his nature glowed with boundless life.

SUNSHINE.

Come, tender sunlight of the spring, and shine
    Through all my thoughts ; my inmost being fill,
    Teaching my heart to glow, and yet be still,
With that victorious quiet which is thine.
Oh that my hand had cunning to combine
    The tints wherewith thou robest copse and hill !
    But I, so rich in love, am poor in skill,
And praise fair Truth, yet may not build her shrine.

But every spirit, worshipping aright,
    Must glory in the gifts that others bring ;
    So would I triumph—not as one apart,
But with the kindred throng who love the light,
    Joying in beauty that transcends my art,
    And mutely dreaming notes I cannot sing.

IN THE GARDEN.

SWEET sounds, and scents, and colours join to woo
    My musing heart to love and reverence;
    A tender and a subtle influence
Comes from each graceful form, each brilliant hue;
Strange power have they, my spirit to imbue
    With thoughts above themselves; for e'en while
      sense
    Adores the Beautiful with joy intense,
The soul, far gazing, only seeks the True.

And ye, fair flowers, translating to my sight,
    In gold or blue the pure uncoloured beams,
Are poets and revealers of the light;
Soon is your message told, your life-work done,
    For all your tints are only passing dreams
Of the eternal splendour of the sun.

YELLOW ROSES.

My sweet sun-tinted roses, faint and fair
   As morning twilight ! though ye soon must fade,
   Still shall ye bloom for me.   I will not braid
Soft leaves and fragile blossoms in my hair,
But for a few bright hours, with loving care
   I strive to paint the golden light and shade
   Wherein each curling petal is arrayed,
And the translucent green your leaf-sprays wear.

So would I keep sweet hopes, that else might die,
   And fragrant fancies, withering too fast,
All fresh delight in earth, and sea, and sky,
And the deep joy, so near akin to grief :
   That from the slumberous garden of the past
I may not lose one sun-reflecting leaf.

JULY, 1878.

LIKE waves that rise and fall, the morning sheen
   Glows between quivering leaves, which fain would
      fling
  Their dust and blight to breezes, murmuring
Sweet May-time legends 'mid the sombre green.
Alas for wistful eyes, that have not seen
   The promised loveliness : for changeful Spring
   Has quickly passed, and summer does but bring
Scorched buds and flowers, that tell what might have
  been.

The trees are dark against the tender blue ;
   A deeper shade has bronzed the purple beech,
But even yet, the red leaves bud anew :
And thus, 'mid barren splendours of July,
   Fresh, brilliant hopes burst forth in glowing speech,
And light some pensive heart before they die.

SUNSET.

THE sun is setting—not in colours gay,
   But pure as when he blazed with noonday heat :
   The upland path is gold before my feet,
Save where long, dancing, poplar-shadows play,
Or arching lindens cast a broader gray :
   This radiant hour, when peace and passion meet,
   Stirs with tumultuous breezes, freshly sweet,
The odorous languor of an August day.

Above is peace ; below is gleeful strife ;
   Aflame with sunshine, battling with the wind,
The trees rejoice in plenitude of life :
A sea of light is sleeping in the west,
   Untroubled light, o'erflowing heart and mind
With that empyreal rapture, which is rest.

SEPTEMBER, 1880.

To still September comes a dream of joy :
   The breath of dying roses in the calm
   And sultry air, seems changed to hyacinth-balm ;
Fresh beams and breezes waken, such as toy
With amorous wind-flowers and May-lilies coy :
   Raise, oh ye birds, a wild conjubilant psalm !
   Autumn has reached the goal, has gained the palm,
And Winter comes not surely to destroy.

Nay, prosperous Autumn ! not for thee shall ope
   May's blossoms ; nor for thy dull ear shall sing
Her choir of birds ; thine own winds whirl away
Thy golden vapours, and thy rich decay,
   Till Winter come, stern pioneer of Spring,
Renewing Earth by terror and by hope.

SONGS BEFORE DAYBREAK.

THE birds are singing, though it is not morn,
   Though in the east no rays of glory shine :
   Made clear by hope, their eyes and hearts divine
That in the dusky twilight, day is born.
Trusting they carol, though the heavens warn
   Their fearless joy with many a threatening sign :
   Though, still untinged with gold, the clouds com-
     bine,
While moans the rain-fraught wind, a voice forlorn.

Yes, wake me with your warbling, happy birds,
   That I may feel, before I see, the day ;
That I may muse of hope, while in my heart
The notes translate themselves in gladsome words :
   E'en plashing rain-drops mingle with your lay,
And in its harmony the wind has part.

THE SEED.

No light of sun or moon can reach the seed
   That blindly in the bosom of a flower
   Ripens through summer, till its living power
Breaks the frail clasp that held it, and is freed :
Yet not with new-found sunshine can it feed
   The embryo life, that lighted but an hour
   Waits long in utter night its glorious dower :
Cold grows the earth, and spring-time shall not speed.

Not as when warm in fragrant gloom it lay,
   But living hopeless, tombed in frost-bound sod,
   Now seems it poorer than the lifeless clod,
That lies above it, open to the day :
   Yet Night shall keep her own, and lose not one,
   And every child of Day shall find the sun.

OCTOBER, 1879.

THROUGH all the dolorous year mine eyes have sought
    The ever-living loveliness that cleaves
    Even to dim grey skies and rain-bent sheaves :
Still is my garden with such beauty fraught,
And bright azaleas flash me back my thought :
    Their sunny flowers are fallen, but the leaves
    Flame gold and scarlet, and my heart receives
Delight more full than spring or summer brought.

And I can twine a rich October crown
    With branchlets of the golden-tressëd birch,
Green cedar plumes, and beech-leaves ruddy brown,
And woodbine gems, of pure translucent red ;
    Even some lonely flowers may cheer my search,
Sweet as new joys that spring when hope is dead.

NOVEMBER, 1878.

THE sky is dim and silent ; lost are mirth,
  Colour, and motion ; e'en the winds are dumb,
  Save for a constant, faint, unchanging hum,
That seems the voice of the despairing earth.
The birds are pining in this wintry dearth ;
  The trees, that rang with carols frolicsome,
  Show dead black branches, fringed with white,
    whence come
No whispered hopes of any future birth.

And yet to me, the season still is fair,
  Though things of joy so sad and cold become :
Majestic stand the trunks and branches bare,
Their lace-like twigs half-seen, half-hid with snow :
  One frost-bit flower, a red chrysanthemum
Tells of the hidden store of life below.

DECEMBER, 1879

Now is the Earth at rest from sun and storm ;
   And stripped of all her gems and vestures gay,
   Gives thanks to Heaven, while weaklings can but
      pray :
In germs of life, uncouth of hue and form,
She feels the glory of the summer swarm,
   And knows December not less rich than May ;
   For she is young as on her primal day,
And still beneath the snow her heart is warm.

All flowers and fruits are folded in her breast,
   Waiting but fuller radiance from above ;
     And she lies dreaming of her destined hour,
All white and still, most like a soul at rest,
     Rich in hid wealth, and strong in secret power,
   Silent with joy, and pure with perfect love.

UNDISCERNED PERFECTION.

BEYOND the realm of dull and slumberous Night
   I long have wandered with unwearied feet ;
   The land where Poetry and Science meet
Streaks the far distance with a magic light :
Fair visions glide before my dazzled sight,
   And shine, and change, and pass with motion fleet,
   But never clear, and steadfast, and complete
In one transcendent brilliancy unite.

I know, the seeming discord is but mine ;
   The glory is too great for mortal eyes,
All powerless to discover the divine
   And perfect harmony of earth and skies :
I know that each confused and tortuous line,
   To fuller sight, in true perspective lies.

L

THE PAINTER TO THE MUSICIAN.

OH, sing once more, nor think your subtle spells
   Are vainly woven for a nature cold,
   Although I kneel not at the shrine of gold
Wherein the spirit of your worship dwells :
For when your voice in tones impassioned swells,
   The hosts of Dreamland are by you controlled,
   And secrets higher than my words unfold
Even to me the perfect music tells.

And your devotion is akin to mine,
   Though I give praise in colour, you in song ;
The self-same goddess, in another shrine,
   Counts me among the servitors who throng
Her outer courts : to Poesy divine
   Our noblest work, our deepest thoughts, belong.

SPEECH AND SILENCE.

When some sweet voice flows forth in foreign speech,
   The soul shines through the words, and makes them
      clear,
   And all we see interprets all we hear,
For smiles and frowns have wondrous power to teach :
And voiceless grief our inmost heart can reach,
   With calm, deep gaze, too sad for hope or fear :
   Our eyes are wet for those who shed no tear,
And lips that Death has silenced, yet may preach.

In stillness we must win our deepest lore,
   Or 'mid the speechless chant of earth and sea :
   Truth is a spirit, bodiless and free ;
Imaged in words, 'tis perfect truth no more,
   For all our lofty visions fade and flee,
And song begins, when ecstasy is o'er.

BEAUTY.

ETERNAL Beauty, Truth's interpreter,
  Is bound by no austere æsthetic creed ;
  All forms of art she uses at her need,
And e'en unlovely things are slaves to her :
And we, whose hearts her lightest breath can stir,
  Must prize her flowers, whoe'er has sown the seed,
  And love each noble picture, song, or deed,
Whose soul is true, although the form should err.

She is God's servant, but the queen of man,
  Who fondly dreams she lives for him alone,
  And while her power is felt through time and space,
Proclaims her priestess of some petty clan,
  Catching but transient glimpses of a face
  Veiled in rich vestures, loved but still unknown.

THE MYSTERY OF LIGHT.

Light, glorious and eternal, that reveals
    All earthly things, itself is secret still ;
    Love, silent king of heart, and mind, and will,
In lustrous mystery his power conceals ;
And many a clouded spirit dumbly feels,
    But knows not, sees not yet, those truths that fill
    With beauty and with joy the dwellings chill
Even of Life that wounds, of Death that heals.

Yet Light, and Love, and Truth are all our own,
    And minister to us, who know them not ;
      Fair hopes, that look like memories, will throng
E'en hearts that live in darkness and alone,
      And seem to chant some half-remembered song,
    The notes recalled, the lovely words forgot.

ILLUSIONS.

Not in the heavens alone is Truth renowned ;
   Sad human hearts, that seem to love her less,
   Even in mutiny her power confess :
We speak in fables, and are compassed round
With poesy, distilling song from sound,
   Colour from light, and hope from happiness ;
   Subliming weakness, yearning, and distress,
To that high faith wherewith our life is crowned.

All fair deceits are prophets of the truth,
   E'en as the desert mirage tells a tale
      Of palms and wells, real, though far away :
The star-bright hopes that light the world's dim youth
   Are not too brilliant, but too silvery pale,
      To sparkle still, when dawns the golden day.

DAY-DREAMS.

FULL oft through some enchanted land I tread,
   Wherein can live no hatred, pain, or fear,
   Where all the heavens with Truth's own light are
         clear,
And Love's own tints o'er all the earth are spread ;
Where, through illumined foliage overhead,
   Swift, bright-winged birds will flash and disappear,
   While murmuring voices from the leaves I hear,
Repeating all my heart in secret said.

Not there I dwell, and yet my home is there ;
   Those flower-grown paths I trod, a lonely child,
Breathing with simple joy the fragrant air :
Lured on by half-seen beauty even then,
With restless feet I roamed from hill to glen,
   By gleaming birds, by whispering leaves beguiled.

MORNING TWILIGHT.

THERE is a time, when all the heart is dumb,
 Too tired for dread of ill, or hope of good ;
 When o'er dull brain and heavy eyelids brood
Shades of dead grief, endured and overcome,
Whose ghostly presence lingering doth benumb
 The constant soul, that gazed with hardihood
 On living evil : in this twilight mood
Even the sun and wind are wearisome.

Yet is their flickering strife but joy begun ;
 For e'en the spectral shades grow faintly bright,
Like night-born mist, half kindled by the sun :
 Then shut not out the breeze, nor bar the light :
Full noon shall glow for him, who will not shun
 Heaven's dazzling joy-break, though tears cloud his
  sight.

SEMELE.

For her who loves a God, all hope must die
  Of sweet familiar joys, that daily move
  A woman's soul ; of gentle cares, that prove
Her free devotion ; of the answering eye,
Where speaks the heart, and hears each mute reply :
  Yes, these and more she lacks ; yet far above
  That earthly home, expands her heaven of love,
And he she worships glows in sea and sky.

She whom the Sun has wooed—for whom his rays
  Have shone but once, unclouded—well may wait
  Through blackest night ; her hope is one with fate :
Let me behold thee, Zeus !   Dispel the haze
  That shields too tenderly my mortal sight :
  If life be darkness, let it cease in light.

THE PRIEST'S PRAYER.

HAVE pity, Lord !   Let me not die alone !
   Though once I dared my fellow-souls to shrive,
   I am unclean ; with pangs of death I strive.
Alas, what healing balm to me was known
For every heart that made its fevered moan !
   But now that *I* am sick, who shall revive
   My hopeless faith, or save my soul alive,
Since that elixir fails, which was mine own ?

Spirit of God, Who dwellest e'en in me,
   Who speakest even by this doubtful breath,
Whether for good or ill Thou set me free,
   Withhold not Truth, although its price be Death :
I faint, I die, in scorching plains accurst,
Let me drink hemlock, if it slake my thirst !

WEARINESS.

TELL me no more, I must not fear to die ;
  Ye waste your words ; not death, but life I dread :
  Oh, to be numbered with the tranquil dead !
For I am tired ; I do but crave to lie
Under the turf ; only for rest I cry ;
  And yet ye bid me turn my weary head,
  And on the scroll that hangs beside my bed
Read of another life, a home on high.

'Tis strange to think I once had power to cope
  With those who hate the Christ, and scorn His
      word ;
    Sore were my wounds ; my triumphs, oh, how few !
  But now, at last, my prayer for sleep is heard :
    Forgive me, Lord !   Thy promises are true,
And yet I have not strength enough to hope.

THE AGNOSTIC'S PSALM.

Oh Thou, who art the life of heaven and earth,
    Eternal Substance of all things that seem ;
    Or but the glorious phantom of a dream
That in the brain of mortal man has birth :
To know that Thou dost live were little worth,
    Not knowing Thee ; yet oft the heart will deem
    That through its inmost deeps Thy light doth stream,
Bestowing peace for grief, calm joy for mirth.

E'en thus rich music enters tuneless ears,
    Tuneless, and all untrained by ordered notes ;
    Yet its ethereal essence inward floats,
And mingling with the secret source of tears,
    Awhile endues the spirit's wistful sight
    With dim perceptions of unknown delight.

TO AMY, ON RECEIVING HER PHOTOGRAPH.

When of some lovely landscape unforgot
  A shadowy sketch I see, my thought divines
  Clear sunshine gleaming through the pencilled lines,
And cool green shade, where seems a shapeless blot :
I know how morning pierced that sheltered grot,
  How noonday glowed between the tufted pines ;
  And even so, your cold grey portrait shines
With tints unseen by those who know you not.

They cannot see the apple-blossom cheek,
  The eyes of midnight blue, the sun-lit hair ;
Grave are the lips, and will not smile or speak :
  And yet to me the pictured face is fair :
I conned that May-tide bloom when last we met,
And all the eye saw then, the heart sees yet.

NIGHT works like Time : hushed is the busy street :
    Grey are the walls, whose yet untarnished red
    Glared in the sun ; for shadows overspread
All hues of earth, that wearied eyes may meet
The restful heavens ; that mortal hearts may greet
    Eternal truth : while darksome paths I tread,
    The light of other worlds is round me shed,
The glow of distant æons guides my feet.

The silent stars my ecstasy control ;
    No daring hopes, no awe-struck fears intrude
Upon the calm rejoicing of the soul :
From sun to sun, from age to age I climb,
    Until for Space I see Infinitude,
And feel Eternity, where was but Time.

MAN needs no dread unwonted Avatar
   The secrets of the heavenly host to show ;
   From waves of light, their lustrous founts we know,
For every gleaming band and shadowed bar
Is fraught with homelike tidings from afar ;
   Each ripple, starting long decades ago,
   Pulsing to earth its blue or golden glow,
Beats with the life of some immortal star.

A life to each minutest atom given—
   Whether it find in Man's own heart a place,
   Or past the suns, in unimagined space—
That Earth may know herself a part of Heaven,
   And see, wherever sun or spark is lit,
   One Law, one Life, one Substance infinite.

TRANSLATIONS.

M

THE KNIGHT OF TOGGENBURG.

From the German of Schiller.

" KNIGHT, with sister's love for brother,
    Dear to me thou art :
Take this love, and ask no other,
    For it grieves my heart :
Calmly coming, calmly going,
    Welcome shouldst thou be,
But these tears, in silence flowing,
    These are strange to me."

To his bosom, dumbly aching,
    Wild the maid he wrings,
Then away in anguish breaking
    On his charger springs ;

From their mountains, where they tarry,
  Calls his Switzers brave ;
On their breast the Cross they carry
  To the Holy Grave.

Wondrous deeds that host undaunted
  Have in fight performed,
Every helmet's plume has flaunted
  Where the foemen swarmed ;
Toggenburg, that name victorious,
  Frights the Moslem train,
But his heart, 'mid triumphs glorious,
  Is not healed from pain.

He has borne a year of sorrow,
  Now can bear no more,
Wins no respite, night or morrow,
  Rides from camp to shore ;
Sees a ship, with canvas flying,
  Joppa's haven leaves,
Home to that dear country hieing
  Where her bosom heaves.

Now the pilgrim nears her castle,
　　Now his knock is heard ;
Woe ! 'tis opened by a vassal
　　With the thunder-word—
"She you seek, to God is given,
　　Veiled before Him bows,
Yestermorn the bride of Heaven
　　Sealed her marriage vows."

Now his father's castle never
　　Shall receive its lord,
Faithful steed he leaves for ever,
　　Helm, and lance, and sword ;
From the Toggenburg down-stealing,
　　Tells to none his name,
'Neath a gown of hair concealing
　　His majestic frame.

And a little hut he raises
　　Looking towards the glade
Where the convent darkly gazes
　　From the linden shade :

Waiting from the morn's first blushing
   Till the sunset shone,
Silent hope his features flushing,
   Sat he there alone,

Towards the convent gazing, yearning,
   Kept for hours his watch,
To his loved one's window turning,
   Till she clinked the latch,
Till the face and form entrancing
   From the window smiled,
Downward o'er the valley glancing,
   Peaceful, angel-mild.

Now rejoicing, healed from sadness,
   Down to sleep he lay,
Woke again with quiet gladness
   At the dawn of day :
So he sat for many a morrow,
   Kept for years his watch,
Waiting mutely, void of sorrow,
   Till she clinked the latch,

Till the face and form entrancing
   From the window smiled,
Downward o'er the valley glancing,
   Peaceful, angel-mild.
So he sat, when morning's brightness
   Dead and cold he met,
With a face of placid whiteness,
   Towards her window set.

THE MAIDEN'S LAMENT.

From the German of Schiller.

THE oak-wood murmurs,
    The sky clouds o'er,
The maiden paces
    The grassy shore ;
The billows are breaking with might, with might,
And she sighs aloud in the gloomy night :
    Her eyes all heavy with sadness :

" The heart is broken,
    The world is void,
With empty pleasures
    My soul is cloyed ;
Thou Holy One, summon thy child above ;
I have lived my life, I have loved my love,
    And revelled in earthly gladness."

" The tears that thou weepest
 All vainly are shed,
No power hath thy plaining
 To waken the dead ;
But tell me, what comforts and gladdens the heart
When the joys of sweet Love must for ever depart ;
 I, the Holy One, bend to thy crying."

" Let the tears I am weeping
 All vainly be shed,
Let my plaining be powerless
 To waken the dead :
The sweetest delight for the sorrowful heart
When the joys of bright Love must for ever depart,
 Is Love's own weeping and sighing."

THE SHARING OF EARTH.

From the German of Schiller.

"'Take ye the world," cried Zeus from Heaven's
    height,
  "Ye sons of men ! I give it all to you,
A heritage in everlasting right ;
  Now share the gift, as brethren do."

Then hasted every hand to grasp its gain,
  And young or old, each claimed his share of good ;
Soon clutched the Husbandman his golden grain ;
  The Squire rode hunting through the wood :

The Merchant bustled, till his wares were stowed ;
  The Abbot chose him generous cobwebbed wine ;
The Monarch barred the river and the road,
  Crying, "The tenth of all is mine."

Late, when the last had long received his share,
  The Poet came, from regions far and dim ;
Too late ! each heritage had found an heir,
  And nought, alas ! was left for him.

" Ah, woe is me ! Of all thy sons, shall I,
  The truest, be forgotten ? I alone ?"
Loud to the ears of Zeus he sent his cry,
  And threw himself before the throne.

" Nay, if in dreamland thou wert pleased to hide,"
  Rejoined the God, " accuse thyself, not me ;
Where, while they portioned Earth, didst *thou*
      abide ?"
  " I was," the Poet said, " with thee.

" Mine eye was fixed on thy celestial face,
  Mine ear upon the harmonies of Heaven ;
If, by thy light entranced, I lost my place
  On Earth, oh, be the fault forgiven !"

" What help ?" said Zeus : " the Earth is given away,
  Mart, greenwood, harvest, these no more are mine ;
But, if thou be content with *me* to stay,
  Come when thou wilt, a home in Heaven is thine

COMFORT IN TEARS.

From the German of Goethe.

Why art thou sad, when all around
   So gay and bright appears?
For plainly in thine eyes are seen
   The traces of thy tears.

" And if I wept in solitude
   The grief is mine alone,
And with the tears that sweetly streamed,
   More light my heart has grown."

Come, let us clasp thee in our arms,
   Thy joyous comrades say;
And there, whatever thou hast lost,
   Weep thy regrets away.

" Ye brawl and bluster, dreaming not
   The secret of my pain;
My grief is not that I have lost,
   But that I long in vain."

Spring boldly up ; for thou art young,
    With speed thy task begin ;
Thine is the age of daring deeds,
    And strength to strive and win.

" Ah no ! 'tis what I cannot win,
    From me 'tis all too far ;
It dwells as high, it gleams as bright,
    As shineth yonder star."

We do not long to reach the stars,
    But glory in their light,
And gaze to heaven in ecstasy
    Each fair and cloudless night.

" I, too, look up in ecstasy,
    By day my watch I keep,
Then let we weep the nights away
    While I have heart to weep."

THE WANDERER'S NIGHT-SONG.

From the German of Goethe.

Thou, who Heaven's angel art,
   Thou, who pain and sorrow stillest,
And the doubly mournful heart
   With a double comfort fillest !
Ah, what weary days I number !
   Why this sad or gay unrest?
Sweetest slumber
   Come, oh come, to calm my breast

EVENING.

From the German of Goethe.

O'ER every mountain height
   Slumber broods,
Scarcely a zephyr light
   Stirs in the woods
    One leafy crest ;
The song-bird sleeps on the bough.
Wait a little, and thou,
    Thou too, shalt rest.

BURY THE DEAD THOU LOVEST.

From the German of Carl Siebel.

BURY the dead thou lovest,
   Deep, deep within thy heart ;
So shall they live and love thee
   Till Life and thou shall part.

So for their risen spirits
   Thy breast a heaven shall be ;
Like angels, pure and shining,
   They go through life with thee.

Bury the life thou livest
   Deep in another's heart ;
So shalt thou live belovëd
   When dead and cold thou art.

SPRING.

From the German of Ernst Schulze.

Oh come, sweet Spring, thy budding flowers unfold ;
   Within the woods awake the song-bird's lay,
   And gloriously adorn thy kingdom gay
With light, perfume, and clouds beflecked with gold.
All trees shall chant in Love's own murmurous tone,
   With Love the stream shall sing, the forest glow :
   My heart, perchance, that home of midnight woe,
Circled with joy, shall deem that joy its own.

Alas for me ! Why sadly, mutely look
   After long-vanished beams, that once were bright ?
   Why call in vain the ghosts of days more fair ?
She who from out my life all gladness took,
   From Springtide, too, has stolen Love's delight,
   And nothing left, save only Love's despair.

THE RUINED MILL.

From the German of Julius Sturm.

THE moon is newly risen,
  I wander through the vale ;
My dreaming eyes are spell-bound
  By radiance sad and pale.

Behind the mill she rises ;
  I watch her silver shield,
And in my heart burst open
  The wounds I thought were healed.

Long since, the wheels have mouldered,
  And roof and door are gone ;
Babbling of days departed
  The glittering stream flows on.

The moon has sunk in darkness,
  The wind is blowing cold ;
Dead is the miller's daughter,
  And I am grey and old.

THE FIR-TREE.

From the German of Luise von Ploennies.

HIGH on that hill thou seest
  A single fir-tree stand;
I sit there every morning
  And gaze across the land.

The stork comes flying swiftly,
  The field with flowers is gay;
But into the world, my sweetheart
  Has travelled far away.

And roses bloom in the garden,
  And they cut the ripened grain;
And still I wait for my sweetheart,
  He yet may come again.

And the leaves have grown so golden,
  The leaves have grown so red;
And if my sweetheart will not come,
  I would that I were dead!

Oh why hast thou, green fir-tree,
   No red and gold array?
Oh, fiery love within me,
   Why dost thou burn for aye?

Oh, fir-tree, dark-green fir-tree,
   Why art thou not sere and old?
Oh, fiery heart within me,
   When, when wilt thou be cold?

THE WELL.

From the German of Paul Heyse.

YES, wayward girl, be cold and shy,
　　From morn till eve lock up thy heart ;
The flashing lustre of thine eye
　　Must still betray how rich thou art.

That legendary tale they tell
　　Comes back, while thus I gaze and think :
In some old city lay a well,
　　Whose virgin waters none might drink.

So deep, so fathomless a well,
　　So wondrous deep, that when they let
A pitcher down, for hours it fell,
　　And had not reached the bottom yet.

A minstrel, wandering through the land,
　　Espied it, as he passed along ;
He took his fiddle in his hand,
　　And played a tune and sang a song.

And hark ! a sound unwonted here,
A rising, rushing, surging, splashing,
Of water sweet, and cool, and clear,
High over the brim exuberant dashing

The minstrel drank a joyous draught,
And all the neighbours shared his glee :
What boundless bliss must he have quaffed,
Whose voice could set the fountain free !

AN EVENING SONG.

From the German of Rückert.

I STOOD upon the mountain
   Before the sun had set,
And saw how o'er the forest
   Hung evening's golden net.

Earth was bedewed with slumber,
   Shed from the clouded sky,
And all the bells of even
   Sang Nature's lullaby.

I said—Oh heart, acknowledge
   The sleep of earth and air,
And with the meadow's children,
   Rest thou from all thy care.

For all the little blossoms
   Their eyelids gently close,
And with a softer motion
   The streamlet's current flows.

And now the sylph, grown weary,
　Under a leaf doth hide ;
The dragon-fly, dew-sprinkled,
　Sleeps at the river-side.

Now in his rose-leaf cradle
　The golden beetle rocks ;
Back to the fold are hasting
　The shepherd and his flocks.

The lark flies earthward, seeking
　His clover-shaded nest,
And in the wood's recesses
　Lie hart and doe at rest.

And he who has a cottage
　There to his rest has lain,
And he who lives in exile,
　In dreams goes home again.

An eager yearning fills me :
　In vain I long to climb
Up to my own true country
　By mountain paths of time.

MY ONLY ONE.

From the German of J. G. Fischer.

THOU knowest well, that thou art all I have ;
   Oh, do not turn thy lovely eyes from me,
   When of the joys of love I speak to thee ;
     For thou art all I have.

Thou knowest well, that thou art all I have ;
   Why wilt thou envying on the blossoms look,
   Withered too soon, and drifting down the brook ?
     Since thou art all I have.

Thou knowest well, that thou art all I have ;
   But oh, I feel that thou wilt soon depart,
   And leave in loneliness this mournful heart
     Though thou art all I have.

FAREWELL.

From the German of Emmanuel Geibel.

ONE goblet more I drink to thee,
   Thou fair and foreign strand ;
No sadder could this parting be
   Wert thou my native land.

Farewell, farewell ! The sails are spread,
   The wind blows fresh and free ;
Its trail of foam the keel has led
   Along the deep-green sea.

Now sinks the sun 'mid islets fair,
   And rose-red shines the sky ;
'Twas in the hut that glimmers there
   We said our last good-bye.

And oh ! how gladly would I stay,
   Thou lovely child, with thee !
In vain ! the vision fades away
   That was so fair to see.

For this is life—to come, to go,
    To haste o'er sea and shore,
The joys of rest awhile to know,
    Then part for evermore.

Loved for a time, forgotten quite,
    But mutely loving yet—
Is it the dazzling sunset light
    That makes my eyes so wet?

'Tis past!　I dash the tear away,
    And joy with grief has flown;
This restless heart, where'er I stray,
    Must beat henceforth alone.

Well, be it so!　Far o'er the main
    The moon's first ray is bright;
The coast recedes—Yet once again,
    My little maid, good-night!

THE BETTER WORLD.

From the German of Hieronymus Lorm.

WHO lives by thought or by belief
   Finds in the World a home of pain,
   But when Religion's might is vain
Reason is strong to vanquish grief.

Religion, in deep midnight furled,
   A better World but prophesies ;
   Reason, with clear and open eyes,
Is in itself a better World.

A MODERN APOSTLE.

A MODERN APOSTLE.

I.

A GARRET room, outlooking on dull streets ;
  A bed, a chair or two, a half-starved fire ;
A little table, with a lamp, and sheets
  Of printed proofs, and many a written quire ;
Bending o'er these, as though they held the sweets
  Of Power or Wisdom, one in mean attire ;
A slender youth, with sallow mobile face,
Quick, dark-browed, nervous—sure, of Celtic race.

You cry, " A common picture !"   Look again—
  A massive forehead shades the features thin ;
The deep-set eyes are like stilettos twain,
  That might transfix a heart grown hard with sin,
Or pierce a clean-edged wound through skull and brain,
  A pathway for the Truth to enter in :
What strange bright soul inspires that body frail ?
Hear if you will, and know young Alan's tale.

He was the prophet of a little sect
    Which deemed itself a plot of favoured ground,
A nursery-garden for the Lord's elect,
    Rich-soiled, high-walled, and sentinelled around
By angel-bands so keenly circumspect
    They challenged every wind of dubious sound,
And quarantined the sunbeams, lest afloat
In any ray should lurk some poison-mote.

And Alan, nurtured from his infant years
    To be a Levite, holy to the Lord,
Took up the ark of God with reverent fears,
    And girded on the spiritual sword ;
He would not flinch before Philistine jeers,
    Nor take the Babylonish spoils abhorred,
Clean would he keep his soul, pure from the stain
    Of thought, of earthly love, of lore profane.

Alas ! not every saint can quite disown
    Those two unsaintly organs, brain and heart,
Nor dwell upon a pedestal of stone
    Until he grow the pillar's counterpart ;
Nor can he by long prayers and fasts atone
    For unregenerate virtues—the black art
Of feeling and of thought is ne'er unlearned,
And spirits come, although the books be burned.

Poor Alan, with the Gael in his hot blood,
  And that insatiate mind, which rather durst
Plunge and be drowned in the full tidal flood
  Of human wisdom, than live on athirst—
Ah ! how could he, though bred from babyhood
  To deem what most he craved a thing accurst,
Dwell in a land of streams innumerous,
And pine a self-afflicted Tantalus ?

A second-hand bookstall was his fatal tree
  Of knowledge, bearing divers kinds of fruit :
Peaches soft-rinded, melting lusciously,
  Yet bitter-flavoured ; on another shoot
Ruddy-cheeked apples, innocent to see,
  But yielding potent cider ; from one root,
It seemed, grew stimulants and anodynes,
Green opium capsules, and rich-clustered vines.

Here Alan read ; at first, the guilt of reading
  Weighed on his conscience ; he would toss all night,
Praying the Holy Ghost to grant him leading,
  And quell or quench this lawless appetite ;
And then for days from that unhallowed feeding
  Would hold aloof, till in his own despite
He turned unthinking down the accustomed street—
The serpent tempted him, and he did eat.

                                        o

Soon he waxed bolder ; could it be a crime
   To learn how men with spirit overcast
Doubted, and told their doubts in prose or rhyme,
   Prating of " Cosmos " or of " Protoplast " ?
What then of Job, rash questioner sublime ?
   What of the weary throned Ecclesiast ?
He reasoned ; thus accomplishing his fall,
For Reason is the Sin Original.

And so at last he shut his eyes and plunged,
   And took whate'er he found, both good and ill
Pale Christianity with Christ expunged,
   Faint Unbelief deploring its own skill,
Great tomes of metaphysic lore, that sponged
   The World away, leaving the lonely Will :
Carlyle he conned, and—guilt of dye intenser !
Dallied with Darwin and with Herbert Spencer.

A thousand thoughts within his head ran riot,
   Shunning at first his Faith, ensceptred long ;
As Rome's old senators, august and quiet,
   Sat on their ivory chairs, and cowed the strong
Victorious Gauls, as by a speechless fiat
   Divine ; till one of that barbarian throng
Stroked a grey beard ; the answering blow began
The slaughter ; weak wrath proved the god but man.

And thus, when Alan's Faith, by touches rude
   Disturbed, in angry tone began to speak,
And let the invading spirits know how crude
   She was in wit, in argument how weak,
What marvel that the unbaptizëd brood
   Taunted and mocked, and smote her on the cheek,
Cast her to earth, discrowned her reverend head,
And left her bleeding, senseless, well-nigh dead?

Yet still she was not slain, and Alan grieved,
   And fain had stanched her wounds and set the crown
On her scarred forehead, and again believed;
   But Reason came and stayed him with a frown,
Saying, "Why crave and yearn to be deceived?
   She who lies low deserved to be cast down;
'Tis Nature's mandate—to the puny rival
Defeat and death: to the more fit, survival."

Yet many times poor wounded Faith uprose,
   But each time paler, fainter, freshly maimed,
And stronger and more valiant grew her foes,
   Their skill more sure, their strokes more truly aimed;
Till tortured Alan, reft of all repose,
   Plagued night and day by fiery thoughts untamed,
Sought, not the Deity on sapphire throne
Circled with elders; but a God Unknown.

It was a broken prayer, a wild appeal ;
   He spoke aloud, nor knew what words he said.
He did not clasp his hands, or bend, or kneel,
   But paced the room with quick uneven tread,
Now hurrying in the tumult of his zeal,
   Now halting, with a pang of sudden dread,
And now he seemed, with fixed gaze, to invoke
Some present Power : and these strange words he spoke :

" My God ! whether thou be my Father too,
   The Father who willed not to take from Christ
That bitter cup, but rather to renew
   His strength to suffer and be sacrificed ;
Or whether the green earth, the heavens blue,
   And men—kings high enthroned, slaves cheaply
      priced—
Be but thy Visions—transient thoughts and themes,
Which thou, the World-Soul, shadowest in thy dreams :

" My God ! if thou dost hear, or if indeed
   Thy Spirit breathes in mine, and prays this prayer—
Thou knowest my pain, my strife, my famished need ;
   For health, love, gladness, let the morrow care,
To-day I hunger for a perfect creed :
   If I be but thy dream, in me declare
Some symbol of the Truth—or let me die,
That, fleeting, I may know the Dawn is nigh.

" Is not this madness ?   Wherefore do I pray
   To my own soul, and cheat myself with hope ?
Seeking for earnest in the Cosmic play,
   Weak victim of an Oriental trope !
And yet, O Truth, whom I blaspheme to-day,
   Because with doubt and dread I scarce may cope,
Reveal thyself, and let thy sole word be—
' Leave all, take up thy cross, and follow me !' "

His deep eyes shone with rapture as he bade
   To Love and Faith, for Hope's dear sake, adieu :
He owned no "great possessions ;" but he had
   Home, friends, a pittance, and from hearers few
Credence devout ; though some looked shrewd and sad,
   And shook their heads, and whispered that he drew
His doctrines from vile books of Babylon,
By scoffers, named Carlyle and Emerson.

Little he cared in that ecstatic hour
   For friendly or for hostile tongues and pens ;
Let the grim Orthodox be starched and sour,
   The dull beasts growl morosely in their dens !
He felt but his own spirit's fervent power,
   Which—by his thought as by a crystal lens
Converged and focussed in one burning spot—
Imaged that Sun, which mortal eyes see not.

A wondrous Vision rose before his sight—
    The Earth in all her glory ; flowers and trees ;
Purple-robed mountain-ranges, every height
    Gleaming like gold ; rich meadows ; boundless seas,
That changed from sapphire to green chrysolite
    And topaz ; in the land and ocean breeze
Life's voices murmured ; scale and fur and wing
Bright glistened ; while Man trod, apparent king.

But as he looked, there passed a stormful cloud
    Athwart the sun, and wakened fiery strife
In heaven ; he heard the waves roar, and the loud
    Thunders ; then deeper gazing, saw how life
Preyed upon life ; how men, ruthless and proud,
    Destroyed their fellow-men with club and knife
And fire-brand ; or by deadlier arms, and fraud
Refined, and smooth hypocrisy unawed.

Yet in the stained Earth and the darkened Sun,
    He saw, by some revealing miracle,
The Eternal Power which makes the Many, One,
    Shining through all ; the Law made visible :
As though this embryo world had just begun
    To quicken with the shaping Principle
Which silently prepares its robe of youth
A body all translucent to the Truth.

Then came a Voice—" Behold what thou hast sought
   So long ; thyself, and Nature's Self, behold !
Thou couldst not spend thy prayers and tears for nought,
   By human pain my Being I unfold ;
I am the end and essence of thy thought,
   The life of all new creeds and symbols old ;
I rule in star and atom ; all mankind
Work out my purpose in their battlings blind.

" But thou, whose eyes are opened ; who dost see
   Thy true Soul, and yet livest—thou, rejoice !
Go forth into the world and speak of me ;
   I choose thee from all men by thine own choice ;
In evil and in good, in bond and free
   I live, and utter truth in every voice ;
Each sings his few faint notes of joy and woe,
Only my Prophets the full concord know."

The Voice passed, and the Vision, and gave place
   To darkness and deep silence, as of death ;
And the young mystic fell upon his face,
   Scarce his heart beat, and scarce he drew his breath :
This glorious message to the human race,
   Unknown to ancient seers, who cried, " Thus saith
The Lord," held all his sense and soul entranced,
While the hours fled, night deepened, morn advanced.

He felt as one who, having grasped the whole
  Of his desire, may rest ; he seemed estranged
From realms of Space, and freed from Time's control,
  Pure Spirit ; not from dream to dream he ranged,
Nor prayed, nor hoped, nor pondered ; for his soul
  Was all concentred in one thought unchanged :
Till slowly he awoke, when dawn was near,
Mortal again ; but God's anointed seer.

II

Small, fragile, and dark-eyed was Alan's mother,
   Of Highland blood ; her solemn Saxon mate
Had ne'er been able quite to quench or smother
   The poet-flame within her breast innate ;
She had been wont, to Alan and no other,
   Strange tales of wraith and kelpie to relate,
And wondrous legends of the second sight,
Claimed by her race as its ancestral right.

She told her tales in rapid whispers, sitting
   Over the fire, with changeful glances wild,
And quick dramatic hands, that wove unwitting
   A spiritual garment for her child,
Who all the while, his bright eyes never quitting
   Her face, beside her crouched, enrapt, beguiled :
But these were secret pleasures : when she heard
A slow step, hushed was the half-spoken word.

For Alan's father, tall, large-boned, and grim,
    Considered works of fiction merely lies,
And banned all poetry except the hymn ;
    His creed forbade him earthly gifts to prize,
Calling mirth, folly—love, a sinful whim :
    Such faith at once contracts and satisfies
The constant soul ; that one ideal spark
Shows all the world around blank, cold, and dark.

Each day he opened with a prayer, and singing ;
    The prayer a little sermon in disguise,
Teaching the Lord His own designs, and slinging
    Smooth pebbles at unwise and overwise ;
The hymn was loud, aggressive, as though flinging
    Contemptuous pearls to neighbours or to spies ;
Like a big drum he sang, beat with small skill ;
Alan, more low ; the mother, clear and shrill.

That morning, Alan sang with fervour double ;
    His inner exaltation overbore
All sad presentiment of toil and trouble
    And severance of old friendships, and welled o'er
In natural song : the hymn said, " Life's a bubble,
    A wave that breaks in foam upon the shore,
A fading leaf :" but Alan's voice rang out
As though its burden were a triumph-shout.

And after prayer, and hymn, and frugal meal,
    He spoke, and all his glorious Vision told ;
At first with painful strivings to reveal
    His secret heart : but soon he grew more bold,
And e'en his father's look could not congeal
    His ardour ; as the petrifying cold
That binds the dull stream, Winter's prisoned vagrant,
Freezes not generous wine, nor ether fragrant.

The old man heard with bony brows drawn down,
    And keen eyes watchful, and thin lips compressed ;
The anxious mother shivered at his frown,
    And trembled for her son, yet unconfessed
Shared in the new belief ; she plucked her gown
    With nervous fingers, while her loving breast
Was rent with fear, and hope, and awe-struck joy
That Heaven had found a Prophet in her boy.

The story ended ; then with look austere,
    And speech deliberate, calm, the father spoke :
" I understand you well ; your words are clear ;
    You fain would cast away the ancient yoke,
Renounce the Lord of Hosts, whom devils fear
    And angels worship ; and, forsooth, invoke
Some newer God, who dwells in rogue and thief,
Yet speaks by you, of his apostles chief.

"Call on your Baal !   Try what he can do—
    Surely he is a god, though he begins
With blasphemy—doubt not—your course pursue ;
    Shout, leap, and wound your soul, till suffering wins
Success ; and then remember, that while you
    Are feasting, I am fasting for my sins,
And wishing Heaven had blotted out the morn
On which a man-child to the world was born."

He broke off with a sob ; Alan, aghast
    At such emotion, hastened to his side,
Crying, " My father !"   But he roughly cast
    His son away, with gestures that defied
Sorrow and pity, and in silence passed
    Out from the house, in his unbending pride
That did brave battle with a love and grief
More deep than aught except his stern belief.

And now the son and mother, each to each
    The best-loved thing on earth, were left alone ;
Then on his knees beside her, without speech
    He fell, and took her cold hands in his own ;
And she, all trembling, weeping the new breach
    Between her dear ones, spoke in faintest tone,
Pleadingly, brokenly, as though she prayed
For grace, that some hard sentence might be stayed.

" My Alan, my dear son ! my heart will break—
　　Although I always knew that God would send
His Spirit—that some morning you would wake
　　And feel that strength was granted you to spend
In some great service—only, for my sake
　　And for your father's, wait a little—bend
Awhile, before his anger—who can tell?
This wrathful mood may pass—he loves you well."

But he replied, " My mother, tempt me not !
　　For you I would do all things—all, save this—
Nay, I could wish my father's wish, to blot
　　My hour of birth, rather than idly miss
My birthright : grieve you that my zeal is hot ?
　　You taught me, by your songs, your tales, your kiss
That human love, that heed of Wisdom's ray,
By which the heavenly Voice I now obey.

" Ah, do not weep, dear mother !　Even those
　.Who cast me forth, shall hear the Word divine ;
To-morrow, in the face of friends and foes,
　　My charge, once held so dear, I must resign—
But weep not !"　He embraced her and arose
　　And went forth, that the April sun might shine
Into his heart, and quiet grief and wrath
And exultation, and make plain his path.

"Twas in an English town that Alan dwelt,
    A town marked Liberal both by creeds and votes,
Where every individual voice did melt
    In the loud hum of Progress ; jarring notes
Of small exclusive sects were merely felt
    Like nettle-stings when dock-leaf antidotes
Are plenteous ; there, the party-leader's cue
Was to hope all things, and believe a few.

Turning a corner sharply, Alan met
    George, an old school-mate, strong in politics,
Ruddy and fair, short-statured and thick-set,
    Well versed in all the rhetorician's tricks ;
An eye he had that you could ne'er forget,
    Blue, humorous, clear ; not steady to transfix
The erring, but most skilful to detect
A meeting's mood, and watch a word's effect.

" "Tis you !" he cried—" we have not met for long ;
    In truth, I wonder you are still alive,
Pacing your treadmill round with weary song,
    Seeking rich honey in a dronish hive,
Boring deep wells Artesian in the wrong
    Strata, whence you may dig, till you arrive
At the earth's core, yet no refreshing drop
You find, till at the central fire you stop.

" Some day, your friends will leave you in the lurch,
   For what know you about the selfish springs
That move them to condemn all true research ?
   Like Gallio, I care nothing for such things—
And yet I care for *you*—I know a church
   Where you might fearlessly unfold your wings,
Read, think, and labour, and perchance do good—
A free church, in a crowded neighbourhood.

" They want a parson now—the salary
   Is poor, but better than your present pay ;
And what is worse than the dull destiny
   Of one condemned, year after year, to stay
Shut in a sect, and preach incessantly
   The same old doctrines in the same old way ?
Come forth, nor heed how bigots may abuse
The step—shake off their dry dust from your shoes."

The words, though kindly meant—the flippant cavil—
   The confident suggestions, like commands,
Jarred upon Alan ; then, he fain would travel,
   And scatter the good seed in many lands ;
Yet might he not, by George's aid, unravel
   Present perplexities, and set his hands
To the Lord's plough ? And would not God enlarge
   His field, if true he were in one small charge ?

Therefore he answered—"Come to-morrow night,
    And tell me of this church—my trust I leave
Not for its dulness, nor for any spite
    Against the people, who in faith receive
My words, and to their utmost power requite
    My service ; nay, I willingly would cleave
To this old home ; but God has called me thence,
    Granting me sight of his Omnipotence."

"Well," said the other—"so that you come out
    I care not why.   On Sunday evening, late,
When none of your good friends will be about,
    And your last sermon will have fixed your fate,
Expect me.   Now, good-bye ; I have to spout
    To-night, at a political debate,
And must begin to think what I shall say—
So, till to-morrow !"   And he went his way.

Then Alan wandered far, beyond the town,
    Past budding hedge-rows, where the spider weaves
Her tracery ; past trees with branches brown
    Seen through their April robe of light green leaves ;
And past bright gardens, where the tulip-crown
    And fruit-buds pink, are spoiled by wingèd thieves ;
Such common sights, and the soft wind's caress
Filled all his soul with strength and happiness.

Farther he rambled ; on through country lanes
   And copses where the ferns their fronds unrolled,
And pastures where the gentle spring-tide rains
   Jewelled anemone and marigold ;
Thrushes and blackbirds carolled joyful strains,
   And all things sang, in cadence manifold—
" Rejoice, rejoice, with bird and tree and flower !
Rejoice, rejoice, in plenitude of power !"

Homeward he turned, his ardent mind sincere
   Feasting on this glad gospel ; soon, ah soon !
The trembling mother must forget her fear,
   The steadfast father must accept that boon
Dearer than rubies ; all should see and hear
   With souls undimmed, exultant in the noon
Of cloudless Truth ; Faith, Hope, and Love, these three,
At last should blend in perfect trinity.

P

III.

ALAN had preached his sermon—grave, devout,
  Yet full of lightnings and electric shocks
For tender souls who reckoned even doubt
  Less damnable than faith unorthodox :
Henceforth the young apostle stood without
  Their iron gates, made fast with bars and locks,
Till his last banishment to realms beneath,
Where scoffers ever weep and gnash their teeth.

But now he sat and chatted in his room
  With his friend George, who comfortably smoked
His pipe, unthinking of so dread a doom,
  And talked in worldly tone, that half-provoked
Alan to wrath ; yet on the tranquil fume
  Floated kind wishes, clad in words that joked,
And many a scheme, by friendly warmth begot,
And pictures quaint of Alan's future lot.

" The people, chiefly poor and ignorant,
   Will be a stony field for you to plough ;
What thoughts they spare from misery and from want
   May they be yours !   But let me show you now
Another aspect : you will have a scant
   Sprinkling of better hearers, to allow
Scope for your genius—men of moderate wealth,
Whose tonic for their spiritual health

" Has been to found a church where all is free,
   The seats, the service, and the preacher's thought,
Where e'en the poorest may behold the Tree
   Of Life, and taste, and eat his fill for nought :
A fine idea, though such things to me
   Are nothings : well, their cleverest member caught
Directly, at your name ; for he had heard
You once, and had remembered every word.

"'Their cleverest, not their richest : though he rules
   The others, he is but a *dilettante ;*
(Our thirty millions, true, are ' mostly fools,'
   Wisdom is rare, and men of mind are scanty !) ;
They reverence him, with faith that never cools
   For having meant to write a book on Dante—
All, save his helpmate ; commonplace and keen,
Through her sage lord her wifely eyes have seen.

"Then their one daughter—did you meet her ever?
    Slim shape, and soft brown hair, and dark-blue eyes,
So gentle, that you scarce believe her clever,
    And quite entrancing, were she not so wise:
But oh, beware of Ella's beauty! never
    Let that Madonna fairness win your sighs;
Or, if you should address her, use your tact,
And study first the sciences exact.

"The heavenly host she watches from her attics,
    She knows the name and place of every star;
True incarnation of Pure Mathematics,
    She cares for all that is abstruse or far:
Go, woo her with Dynamics and with Statics,
    And term your love a force molecular;
She then, perchance, may fathom your intention—
Plain language is beneath her comprehension.

" Enough of this! you are a son of God,
    And do not haunt the daughters of the earth—
Yet who can tell? you are no frozen clod;
    Perchance fair Venus, whose celestial worth
You long have slighted, may prepare a rod
    To torture you, or else a cup of mirth
To tempt you—Well, I hope 'twill be the latter:
As to the church, be easy, for that matter

" Is practically settled.   Now, good-night,
  And happy dreams of—whatsoe'er you choose !"
They parted.   Alan, by the fire's dim light
  Long meditated on the hopeful news,
And felt that he unthankfully should slight
  Heaven's leading, could he hesitate to use
A proffered chance of free unfettered work,
Came it from Jew, or Infidel, or Turk.

And then he looked from out his window high,
  As though the fresh night air could put to proof
His purity of heart : against the sky
  Each house stood black, distinct, and each wet roof
Gleamed in the moonlight ; tapering slenderly
  Rose many a spire : the city seemed aloof
From care and toil ; and said, by silence deep—
" Doubt not nor ponder, but in gladness sleep."

Why should I weary the long-suffering Muse
  And listener patient-souled, with tedious telling
Of letters, of official interviews,
  Of change of ministry, and change of dwelling,
And how the fond proud mother wept to lose
  Her son, and how the father's heart was knelling
The death of hope, or how the elders prayed
In vigorous language for the renegade ?

Enough, that Alan found himself installed
   In his new church, and gloried in the sense
Of working unimpeded, unenthralled ;
   Here was no sentinel, demanding "Whence
Come you, and whither go ?"   A town unwalled
   Was that society, with no defence
Save the united force of Faith and Science—
In truth, a somewhat perilous alliance.

Here he proclaimed the Brotherhood of Men—
   God lives in all ; by Him are all inspired,
And so are equal ; to the Prophet's ken
   The king is level with the drudge o'ertired,
And what he is, should seem : with tongue and pen
   He preached Equality, until he fired
His people ; and ere long, the novel schism
Was christened " Pantheistic Socialism."

Such was his lot, when first I bade you look,
   Kind listener, at his study, where he wrote
His deep thoughts in a world-convincing book ;
   But that was night—his days he would devote
To patient work in many a squalid nook,
   Amid such sights and odours, as denote
The homes of women dulled in heart and eye,
Mothers of starveling babies, born to die,

Or for worse fates. Such wretches he would aid
   From his own scanty income ; sometimes even
They ventured in to hear him, half afraid,
   And did not understand, but felt near heaven :
Of motley stuff his little flock was made,
   Rich men, poor men, and beggars, with a leaven
Of gentle women ; but for him, the place
Contained but one, with sweet Madonna-face.

The blue eyes gleamed with quivering light, as though
   Some lamp within had just begun to shine,
The pale cheeks flushed, as 'mid the latest snow
   Bloom faint pink almond blossoms—welcome sign
Of coming Spring—he deemed this changeful glow
   Enkindled by an intuition fine
That pierced through speech and symbol, ne'er content
Until it knew the soul of what he meant.

He watched the face on Sundays, dreamed of it
   Through all the week ; in haunts of dark distress
And sordid shame, he saw its beauty flit,
   Now, for a moment, calm and passionless,
And now again with sudden radiance lit,
   Like some new-born diviner consciousness
Evolving from completed human grace
The future parent of a nobler race.

No Raphaelite Madonna has a brow
    Like Ella's, nor could e'er have learnt the use
Of sciences to which by voiceless vow
    Her strength was dedicate ; in themes abstruse
She locked herself, and scarce had craved till now
    A truth not yielded by her life recluse ;
As little children, miserably fed,
Grow faint, but are not hungry for their bread.

For she, with innocent clear sight, had found
    That those about her merely thought of thinking,
And felt they ought to feel ; with quick rebound
    She drew her life away from theirs, and shrinking
From windy verbiage, craved some solid ground,
    Trying to satisfy her soul by linking
Truths abstract ; no vague talk of liberal views
Can alter cosine and hypotenuse.

Her mother, with shrewd mind of meaner class
    Laughed inly, when she heard some " thinker " draw
The wonted music from his sounding brass,
    Showing that with approval Christ foresaw
This nineteenth century of steam and gas,
    And Mammon, and " Inexorable Law,"
Or wresting from St. Paul a strong opinion
In favour of the theory Darwinian.

But Ella grieved ; her father's lucubration
   On Dante (which, in sooth, till Doomsday comes
Shall never be writ down)—the declamation
   Of pseudo-scientific Chrysostoms
Rejoiced her not ; she gained a reputation
   For gentle chillness ; and, since nought benumbs
The heart so much as when our friends suppose
It cold, poor Ella slowly, sadly froze.

Yet Ella was a woman, and the frost
   Bound not her inmost nature ; still she kept
The natural love for children ; she had lost
   A baby sister once, and when she slept
Often the little child's white image crossed
   Her dreams, and nearer stole to her, and crept
Close to her heart ; then, piercing through her sleep
Remembrance thrilled, and she would wake and weep.

When Alan came, at first she only smiled
   At his fresh ardour ; yet she oft would check
Her satire ; for he seemed a very child,
   Pure, single-minded, with no marring fleck
Of self-conceit, although by dreams beguiled ;
   And she would sigh, to think how time must wreck
His hopes, and all his fancies disenchant ;
So mused the girl, like some old maiden aunt.

But soon, a strange new light began to break
   Upon her mind, and dubiously to fall
O'er thought and feeling : what if the mistake
   In truth, were hers ; and what if after all
This visionary seer were more awake
   Than she, the sage and mathematical?
'Twas thus she pondered, as in church she sate
Listening, with changeful colours delicate.

From pitying, she began to sympathise,
   From sympathising, almost to revere ;
The inner light grew radiant in her eyes,
   And she forgot her wise predictions drear,
And she forgot to carp and criticise,
   And all things she forgot, except to hear,
And hope, and with a willing mind receive
The mystic word—and lastly, to believe.

Her face grew fairer, and her step more light,
   As though she entertained, not unaware,
An angel : as some holy anchorite,
   When heavenly visitants have deigned to share
His hut and food, will feel a sweet delight
   Henceforth, in water pure and meagre fare ;
So Ella found new pleasures in her home,
And fresh gradations in Life's monochrome.

More bright and blithe she was, than any yet
    Had known her ; all around might well discern
The change, much marvelling what amulet
    Transformed the gentle maiden taciturn
So gladsomely. When she and Alan met,
    As soon they *must* meet, haply might she learn
The spirit of all prophets who have dwelt
On earth, and dream what Christ's apostles felt.

IV.

AT last they met, once, twice, and many times,
  Until she knew the secret of his being,
That essence which an ardent zeal sublimes
  From the dull ashes ; faith was slowly freeing
Her soul from fear ; she felt as one who climbs
  High peaks at midnight, knowing, but not seeing
The depths beneath him, while his lantern's glow
Shines brilliantly before him on the snow.

What shall the sun reveal ?   A cloud-robed world,
  A space of white about the traveller's feet,
And all things else impenetrably furled
  In vapours cold ?   Or will the mist retreat,
Unveiling valleys green, with lakes impearled,
  And bounded by a curve of Alps, that greet
The dawn with rosy summits, towering high
Beneath the paling moon and faint blue sky ?

But Alan —with heart pure and passionate
   That ne'er of any woman's love had dreamed,
To noble service ever consecrate—
   Now joyed in broadening, brightening noon, that
      streamed
Above him and around, till Life and Fate
   Were nought but one glad radiance, and Love seemed
The fruit of Truth's white flower, grown sweet and ripe ;
Nay, Truth herself was here, the perfect type

In a fair woman's form ; the one Ideal
   Shining all glorious 'mid the figures grey
Of Earth ; how different from the hideous Real
   He saw in court and alley day by day !
He was of those who going down to Sheol
   Can find God there, yet none the less do pray
To see Him, not through veils of shame and vice,
But as man first beheld in Paradise.

Yet when the Truth is clad in beauteous flesh
   That man may know it, human love will claim
Its rights ; and daily deeper in the mesh
   Sank Alan's heart, and all his fine-strung frame
With passion throbbed.   One August evening fresh
   He walked in Ella's garden, while the flame
Of sunset lit the trees with golden sheen,
Changing to chrysoprase their sombre green.

And she was at his side ; he spoke to her
   Eagerly, earnestly, and yet he said
No word whose mere significance could stir
   The pulse ; but every syllable, instead
Of telling its own tale, was messenger
   Of Love ; and answering came the fitful red
To Ella's cheeks ; though, as they slowly walked,
'Twas but of Alan's mission that they talked.

Until he said, close-bending, "When at first
   I came, and saw the rows of faces blank,
The brutish and the ignorant, and worst
   The self-complacent rich, my spirit sank
A moment ; then a flood of sunshine burst
   Upon me, for I saw your eyes that drank
The message, and returned it richly bright,
As this deep rose gives beauty to the light.

" And as the rose within her petals hides
   The rays which they reflect not, yet receive,
Oh, tell me now that in your heart abides
   Full confidence—nay, Ella, do not grieve,
Look up—assure me that one Vision guides
   Your steps and mine—that you in truth believe :
I know it, yet forgive me if I seek
To hear it—Ella ! speak to me—oh speak !"

She faltered " I believe " with head low-drooped,
    And tearful eyes—new longings and alarms
Athwart her inward vision swiftly trooped ;
    As one whom unfamiliar music charms
Breathless and mute she stood ; but Alan stooped
    And kissed her lips, and clasped her in his arms,
Crying, " I love—I worship you !   We share
One life—oh joy too great for man to bear !"

And she replied ; such answers are not made
    In speech articulate ; no word she spoke
For Alan's ears, but on his breast she laid
    Her head, as though she sought at once to cloak
And to express her passion.   They had stayed
    Thus, for long hours, but that a loud sound broke
Upon their rapt communion, like the knell
Of that bright moment—'twas the evening bell

For prayer.   They hurried in, nor watched the glow
    Of sunset fading from the purple beech,
And, bidding fond good-night, she bade him go,
    That she, with chosen words, might try to reach
Her parents' hearts, before she slept.   And so
    The sacred love-tale was profaned by speech,
Till from the two she won a slow consent,
Mingled with scolding and with merriment.

The father, half in earnest, half to tease,
    Exclaimed—" Just like Cadijah and Mahomet,
Or Beatrice and Dante—whom you please !
    I wish you joy, my daughter, and your comet
Is brilliant."   The shrewd mother, ill at ease,
    Said "No—your will-o'-the-wisp !   What *can* come
        from it ?
And what's the use of all your Conic Sections
If like a fool you yield to your affections ?"

But Ella gloried in the grudging " Yes ;"
    Love lent the charmëd days bright plumes to fly,
Woke her each morn, and filled her loneliness
    With light, and sang at eve her lullaby :
Yet, as the spring-buds burst, her joy grew less—
    No chill distrust of Alan's constancy,
Nor any fear that time could e'er abate
His fervid love, made her disconsolate.

It was not this ; but her deep-thinking brain
    Learned slowly, mournfully, against her will,
How mystic faiths are woven from a vain
    Tissue of dreams, which hold men captive still
In day-light ; and she saw, with bitter pain,
    That every thought, deed, passion, good or ill,
Might thus be sanctified, and at its need
Find refuge in some hospitable creed.

And when she conned the pages of his book,
   And saw his cherished thoughts, all printed clear,
Robbed of that glow suffused of voice and look
   Which made their mellow misty atmosphere,
She shivered, almost thinking she mistook
   The words, that seemed so living to her ear,
So spectral to her eye—men praised the style,
Bold, fiery : mute she heard, with pallid smile.

Not that her love diminished—nay, it grew :
   As oft from wild delirious words we know
The spirit's beauty, so his nature true
   Shone out more bright through the delusive show
Of gloaming fantasies ; but well she knew
   Her Reason tipped the dart, and strung the bow,
To slay his Passion : with a wife to dwell
Not wedded to his soul, for him were Hell.

Confute a theologian ; with sharp word
   He answers you, yet may forgive the thrust
If he be quite convinced that you have erred :
   But tell Jehovah's prophet that his trust
Is nought—he will not rage, but he will gird
   His loins in silence, and will shake the dust
From off his feet, and go his lonely way,
Over dry desert sand, or fenlands grey.

                               Q

She pined with strange distress—the woman's heart
    Throbbed, quivered, bled ; while the logician's mind
Worked on relentless, heeding not the smart,
    Ne'er to be drugged, or deafened, or made blind :
Against herself her riven self took part,
    The martyr and the torturer combined :
Stretched on the rack, bound with flesh-cutting rope,
What is the poor maimed anguished victim's hope ?

What is a woman's hope when she is torn
    By passion and by thought, and cannot cease
To think or love, nor teach herself to scorn
    Her deepest life, nor ever win release
From the harsh yoke, too heavy to be borne,
    Of iron principles that crush her peace :
Will not some opiate give her dreamful rest
Till she return to the Great Mother's breast ?

Nay ! rather let her maim her shrinking soul —
    That groping she may climb her lame way in
To Life—than down to Death, seeing and whole,
    Spring, damned by the inexpiable sin
Of treachery ; and in the longed-for goal
    Find that fair-seeming Heaven which traitors win,
Whose gate is bliss ; whose midmost point, a germ
Of Hell, whence issues the undying worm.

'Twas a May twilight—and the two once more
- Paced round the walks where they were wont to spend
Sweet hours : but Ella spoke as ne'er before—
   Calmly, as one who, dying, tells his friend,
His best-belovëd friend, that life is o'er,
   That now is come the dead, blank, hopeless end ;
Yet weeps not, neither moans, because his breath
Is well-nigh quenched by the chill winds of Death.

But Alan stayed her—"No, it cannot be !
   This is some fevered nightmare dream !" he cried—
" Wake and believe, dear Ella ! wake and see
   How Earth and Heaven by God are glorified ;
His presence shines in every flower and tree,
   And in ourselves—and shall He be denied
By those who breathe His Spirit ?   Be not you
Like the blind throng, who know not what they do !

" Forgive me, Dearest ; you are sad and pale ;
   I speak too harshly."   But she answered—" Nay,
Be not so gentle, lest your words avail
   Too much—lest I be tempted to obey
Love, and not conscience : my resolve is frail,
   Yet I *will* speak : oh turn your eyes away,
And do not touch my hand, the while I try
To tell my thought—until we say good-bye.

"You are as true as any seer of old,
    Prophet, or martyr; you would sell your life
That Faith might rise up from her torpor cold,
    And vanquish doubt, hypocrisy, and strife:
For this I loved you—yes, long ere you told
    Your love—yet, Alan, if I were your wife
I should be but a mist, a leaden cloud,
Folding your spirit in its clinging shroud.

"For all my faith is gone, that seemed so sure
    Even that God who every day is wroth
With sinners, gives a refuge more secure
    For the sad heart; the banquet is of froth
Which you in mercy set before the poor,
    Not knowing: Alan, Alan, that we both
Might strive to find, by patient thought and search,
Some firm foundation for a nobler Church!"

Her voice grew stronger, and more clear her glance,
    As thus she pleaded, and to thoughts long pent
Within her breast, gave language; she perchance
    Clung to some hope: but Alan, eloquent,
Broke forth with all the story of his trance,
    And how he was inspired of God, and sent
To tend the flame Divine 'mid vapours damp
And cold—the dim yet ever-burning lamp.

She listened—then she said, in tones that fell
   Upon his soul and senses heavily—
" Long have I pondered o'er this vision-spell ;
   For me it holds no magic.   You are free,
And we must part—kiss me and say Farewell.
   Yet are you mine to all Eternity—
No other voice or look my heart can move,
I love you with irrevocable love."

The pallid mournful face, the solemn tone,
   Slew all his hope.   He clasped her to his breast,
And kissed the passive lips, that chilled his own
   Like icicles, and speechlessly expressed
Her anguish—till she cried, with sudden moan
   Thrusting him from her—" Leave me—it is best—
I am too weak to bear it."   Forth he went
Alone, with quick blind steps, and head low-bent.

When some poor lonely pilgrim devotee
   Who worships in the temple of a saint,
Coming one morning with his fervent plea
   Finds the shrine empty—trembling then and faint
He leaves the stone, deep-printed by his knee,
   And goes out homeless, with no wild complaint,
But stricken.   Yet to feel what Alan felt
Is sharper pain—to see the spirit melt

And fade and vanish from some image fair
　　Of Truth, whose glory clothed it like the sun,
But now departs, leaving it cold and bare
　　And lifeless.　One dark moment, only one
He doubted his Ideal ; but his prayer
　　And answering Vision, came afresh, and spun
A web, that nought could break except the power
Of Life's last sad illuminating hour.

And Ella ?　Almost stupefied with woe,
　　Of *him* were all her thoughts, as bowed, forlorn,
He left her, sorely wounded, as a foe
　　Can never wound.　She scarce could stay to mourn
Her own maimed life, but, pacing to and fro,
　　Pictured his days of weary labour, shorn
Of joy ; until the bitterness of loss
O'erwhelmed her, and she stooped to take her cross.

She set herself to suffer and endure
　　In silence.　Life, though mutilated, marred,
Must yet be lived ; there was not any cure,
　　Nor any further stab ; the gate seemed barred
Alike to hope and fear, and she was pure
　　At least, of treason ; yet the thought was hard
That this last act of loyalty could gain
Nought from her Love, save haply his disdain.

Heart-sore, all probing hints she sought to parry,
   But when at length she spoke, her father said—
" My dear, a man of genius should not marry,
   It should be penal for a seer to wed ;
You know, Ezekiel's wife must help to carry
   His ' burden.' "   " Yes, and help to earn the bread,
And bake it," said the mother—" glorious fate
No doubt—for ' glorious ' means ' unfortunate ' !"

V.

Summer passed by, and Autumn ; Winter came
  With grey cold days and black unpitying nights,
And many children gathered round the flame
  Of Yule-tide logs, and dreamed of new delights
With the New Year : many, with shivering frame,
  Half-naked, famished, crept to see the sights
In gay shop-windows—a celestial treat !
On earth there might be bread, and sometimes meat,

But this was Heaven.   They had their make-believe,
  For every child can find an open door
Even from Hell, and thoughtlessly achieve
  Proserpine's miracle ; while she who bore
The starvelings, crouches too benumbed to grieve
  In her cold room, and sees but the bare floor
And fireless hearth, and hungers through the day,
Idle, or toiling hard for paltry pay.

Wages were low that winter ; work was scant ;
   And many little groups of men would cluster
Round the street corners ; grim they were and gaunt,
   With hollow cheeks and sunken eyes lack-lustre ;
And oft, attracted by the ready rant
   Of some stump orator, a throng would muster
To hear of wrongs and rights, and pass a plan
For straightway equalising man and man.

And Alan went among them ; he was pale
   And thin as they, but his deep eyes outshone
With self-consuming light, that told a tale
   Of Hope and Love irrevocably gone,
But Faith still clinging to her Holy Grail—
   That sacred poison-wine, which made him wan
And fiery, giving strength to brave and bear
All ills, all woes ; strength even to despair.

But at the people's groan, his heart waxed hot,
   And loathed the miserable prayers and pence
He had to give, and private pangs forgot
   In the one sorrow of his impotence
To succour ; he would say he scarce knew what
   In fire-words, winged with fatal eloquence,
And then go home, and in his study brood
Through night, till dawn, careless of sleep and food.

Thus the drear days dragged on ; and with the spring
    No comfort came, but rather woe more keen,
For Poverty more deeply plunged her sting,
    And stalwart frames grew slouching, pinched, and lean,
And there arose that sullen murmuring
    Which may mean little, but perchance may mean
The roll of coming thunder, and the flash
Of lightning—or the earthquake's deadlier crash.

One day, as Alan sat intently writing
    An earnest tract on Dives and his dogs,
A sudden tumult, as of fire or fighting,
    Pierced through the smoky mist which ever clogs
The air of towns ; he heard a voice inciting
    To deeds of vengeance—" Are you stones or logs ?
Prove yourselves men !   Burst on them like a flood--
The rich, who batten on your flesh and blood !"

He started up ; that moment, his old friend
    George rushed in, crying—" Quick ! the mob ! a riot !
The people cried for bread, and we who tend
    Their souls political, replied ' Be quiet !
Hope on !' while such as you, the case to mend,
    Fed them on too inflammable a diet ;
And so, among us all, the mischief's done,
The fire brand lit, the rioting begun.

" But now, make haste ! for some of them have taken
   The road to Ella's home—don't turn so white !
Perhaps they'll only ask for bread and bacon,
   And beer, their one inalienable right ;
Cheer up, my friend ! I know you are forsaken,
   But here's a chance to act the doughty knight,
Boldly to face the many-headed giant,
And hold your Love 'gainst all the world defiant !"

They chose the quiet streets, where the fierce rabble
   Came not ; all doors were barred, all shops were shut.
No children in the gutters dared to dabble,
   No woman chatted with her neighbour ; but
From the great thoroughfares they heard the babble
   Of many voices ; once, the fog was cut
By springing flame, and the friends faster strode,
Winding through bye-ways to that dear abode.

Alan, impatient, fevered, onward urged
   His comrade ; they came nearer to the noise,
And in a fair broad road at last emerged,
   Filled with a ragged rout of men and boys
And women ; like a stormy sea it surged,
   That blindly, deafly, ruthlessly destroys :
Some carried stones ; some, staves ; some, iron crows
And rails ; some, bludgeons, fit for deadliest blows.

Some faces were pale, wolfish ; some on fire
  With drink, and hope of spoil or forced largess
From wealthy homes ; in tawdry torn attire
  The women scarcely hid their nakedness ;
And there were jests, foul as the city mire
  Whose old stains clung to many a tattered dress :
Such was the tide that towards the suburb rolled
Where Ella dwelt.   One moment, speechless, cold,

Stood Alan : then, with sudden leap, he sprang
  On a low wall, and beckoned to the crowd
That fought, broke windows, trampled gardens, sang
  And swore, around him ; but his voice rose loud,
And through the clamour like a trumpet rang :
  Its clear bold accents for a minute cowed
The people ; or perchance they thought he came
To spur them forward to their desperate game.

" My friends !" he cried, " all human hopes and lives
  Are truly one ; no man can harm another
But blindly with his proper Self he strives,
  His own soul in the body of his brother :
In you, in all, the spark of Truth survives—
  Is there no father here, is there no mother,
No husband, wife or friend, who knows the tie
Which makes two beings one until they die ?

"That tie is but an image and a sign
    Of universal kinship—to reveal
How men are sharers in the life Divine :
    Think not the rich man's woe the poor man's weal !
When the brain languishes the heart must pine ;
    To hate is atheism, and to steal
Is sacrilege ; to murder, suicide :
I too have erred, who should have been your guide ;

"Oft I spoke rashly, for my heart was sore
    To see you suffer ; humbly I avow
My fault, my crime—Ah help me to restore
    The peace I troubled ; let me lead you now
Back to your homes."   Then rose an angry roar,
    And a great stone struck Alan on the brow,
He staggered ; and before his friend could bound
To save him, he fell prone with heavy sound.

George raised him in his arms—bleeding, death-white,
    Unconscious—then to face the crowd he turned :
"This is the man who laboured day and night
    For you and for your children yes, he burned
His life away, and loved you in despite
    Of all ingratitude, and still returned
Good for your evil—his own wants denied
For you—that you might live, he would have died.

" And you have slain him.   Help me, some of you,
　　To stanch his wounds—those whom he visited
When they were ill, and brought them aid—those, too,
　　Who starved, until he gave them his own bread—
And if by chance there should be here a few
　　Who were in prison, and he came and said
Kind words of hope—'tis only these I pray
Now for their help to carry him away

" And bear him to his friends."   The crowd was hushed.
　　But he who seemed the chief, a strong tall man,
Came forth with halting step, and features flushed,
　　And look half-shamed, half-sorry, and began—
" The parson nursed me when my foot was crushed,
　　I would not do him harm.   Here, Ned and Dan,
Help us to carry him—and you, John, go
Quick, for a doctor—'tis an ugly blow,

" But worse have mended."   Now the throng, subdued
　　Almost to soberness, his words obeyed,
Seeming a funeral pageant motley-hued :
　　As once through Florence paced a cavalcade
Of skeletons and spectres—all the brood
　　Of Famine and of Death—such show they made ;
And bearing Alan in procession grim
Straightway to Ella's home they carried him.

They passed fair gardened homes that rich men build,
   But every man was hidden, as a rat
Hides in his hole ; like birds affrighted, stilled
   By coming storm, crouched those who " eat the fat
And drink the sweet," that Scripture be fulfilled—
   On, till George saw the house where Ella sat
Alone, for both her parents were away,
Spending in Rome their Easter holiday.

She all the day had shivered in suspense
   For Alan's safety, growing sick with fear,
And making now and then a vain pretence
   To read, but straining all the while her ear,
And starting at each murmur, to see whence
   The voices came ; for as they grew more clear
She felt, she knew, that Alan must be nigh,
To turn the rabble backward, or to die.

There came a roar—she shuddered—then a lull—
   She waited at the window, in her dread,
And soon she heard again the murmurs dull,
   And saw at last a strange procession, led
By men who bore some burden pitiful—
   Was it a comrade, wounded—dying—dead ?
But knew she not the figure and the gait
Of Alan's friend ? Oh Heaven ! Came they too late,

And did they bring him dead, that she might see
　　His face, and weep with unavailing woe?
Nearer they came and nearer—Yes, 'twas he—
　　Her cheeks turned white, her heart stood still, as though
She too must fall; but, tottering dizzily,
　　She left her room in piteous need to know
The truth—with quivering hands unbarred the door,
And ran to meet the crowd, and what it bore.

George saw her coming in her breathless haste,
　　With wide eyes, feet that terror seemed to spur,
Long hair unknotted, floating to her waist;
　　Till then, he scarce had spent a thought on her,
But now he groaned; 'twere easier to have faced
　　A furious mob; he felt a murderer:
Forward he stepped, and lest her strength should fail,
Stayed her, and told, as best he might, the tale.

" He is not dead!" she cried—" not dead!" and then
　　Her heart grew stronger; Alan's face she saw
And scarcely trembled; to those rugged men,
　　Those hungering, thirsting breakers of the law,
She spoke, with accents that seemed alien
　　To her own voice; they listened half in awe,
And bore him to the house; and then dispersed
With money for their hunger and their thirst.

Alan lay still unconscious ; months of toil,
  And care, and grief, had done their work by stealth ;
The mental and the physical turmoil,
  The evil deeds of poverty and wealth,
The city's filth and crime, that could not soil
  His spirit, drained away his body's health :
" But he will live !" cried Ella, fain to grope
For light. The surgeon said, " There still is hope."

" There still is hope." Thus sounds the first low note,
  The first faint tremor of the passing bell !
" There still is hope." The dread that loomed remote
  Draws near ; the poison-pang we sought to quell
Stings sharper for this futile antidote :
  So heavy on her ears the comfort fell—
" There still is hope." She watched his sighing breat',
Feeling herself the very pains of death.

R

VI.

Ella kept anxious vigil by the bed:
　　How strange it is to watch through creeping hours
A face which was Thought's temple, and instead
　　To find blank nothingness, or jarring powers:
For mind, and soul, and senses, all are fled,
　　And weirdly wander in a world not ours,
Some Tartarus, whereof we seek the key,
Striving to follow and to set them free.

Ere night, there came a change; for Alan woke
　　From torpor to delirium; now he seemed
To see again his Vision, and invoke
　　With prayer, some Power divine; anon, he dreamed
Of his old home and his old faith, and broke
　　Into sad cries of "Mother!" and there streamed
From his hot lips full many a wonder wild
Of elves, and wraiths, and witches who beguiled

The hearts of chieftains.   Then he wandered back
   From childish days, and softly moaned the name
Of Ella ; or he trod his wonted track
   'Mid squalor and disease, and vice and shame,
Crying, " I cannot eat while others lack,
   I eat their flesh !"   But still again he came
To that old home, and raved with strange despair
Because he could not find his mother there.

And Ella listened ; these lamentings moved
   Her inmost heart ; her sorrowing eyes grew dim
With bitterer tears—this woman she had loved,
   Tenderly loved, when first betrothed to him,
But, at the severance, haply it behoved
   A prophet's mother to resent the whim
That harmed her idol ; and the two, estranged,
For many months no greeting word had changed.

And who would tell the mother ?   She must come ;
   But who would say to her—" Your son is lying
Wounded to death—he wakes from swoonings dumb
   To rave and moan—perchance he may be dying
E'en while I speak."   Poor Ella, cold and numb,
   Pondered of this, and felt her heart replying—
" You, you must bear the message—only you
Have wrecked his life—take anguish as your due.

As thus she mused, George entered.   "Go awhile,"
  He said, "and sleep, for you are tired and worn,
And I will watch."   She gave a faint wan smile
  At thought of sleep, with this envenomed thorn
Deep in her breast—better the weary mile
  To Alan's home—better to greet the morn
With wakeful eyes, than half to see its beams
In the sad Limbo of unslumbrous dreams.

But forth she went ; and loitering at the gate
  She saw that stalwart limping rioter
Who championed Alan 'gainst the blinded hate
  Of the brute mob.   No tumult was astir,
But only this one man had come to wait
  For news.   In whispering tones he questioned her,
As though a louder sound the ear might reach
Of him who heard but his own babbling speech.

And when she told her errand, he besought
  That he might guide her through the darkening streets,
For some of those who swore and robbed and fought
  That morning, were not sated with their feats ;
He had no fear—*he* never would be caught
  By any slow policeman on his beats ;
She would be safe with him—for well enough
His face was known to every city rough.

So, with her strange companion, Ella wound
　Through many streets, with foot that could not tire,
And scarcely saw the wrecks that lay around,
　The havoc wrought by pillage and by fire ;
Nor did her speed grow slack, until she found
　Her goal ; and then, refusing gift or hire,
Her guide departed ; timidly she knocked,
And a slow trembling hand the door unlocked.

And Ella stepped into the homely room
　Where, two years past, Alan his Vision told ;
There, sitting upright in the fire-lit gloom,
　Was the grey father, stern yet unconsoled,
Still mourning for his son's eternal doom :
　The careworn mother, thinner than of old,
Flitted from spot to spot, or crouching sate
Like a poor bird with nest made desolate.

I know not how the story was begun,
　Nor ended how ; the father's face, hard-set,
Just quivered—"Lord," he said, "Thy will be done !"
　But with reluctant tears his eyes grew wet,
Oozing like drops of blood—"My son, my son !"
　He murmured, seeming all things to forget
Save sorrow ; but the mother, pallid, fierce,
Gazed at the girl, as though she fain would pierce

Her heart. "Your fault!" she cried—"it is your fault !
  His blood be on your head, if he must die ;
Like the proud Pharisees, who did exalt
  Their barren lore, and shouted 'Crucify !'
You slew my son !"   But now the tear-drops salt
  Choked her mad words ; and Ella made reply
By kneeling at her feet and weeping—"Nay,
Mother ! it was myself I meant to slay."

She kissed the slender hand, by toil made hard,
  And the poor mother, seeing her so mild,
And feeling the hot tears, her heart unbarred
  With quick repentance for those plainings wild ;
Saying—"Forgive me—kiss me—I should guard
  My lips from evil. Take me to my child."
The women clung together ; then the three
Set out on their sad errand silently.

They neared the house with many a wordless prayer,
  And knew not whether that they came to seek
Were life or death : George met them on the stair
  With mien so haggard, that it seemed to speak
All that they dreaded ; but he said, " Prepare
  To see him—he is conscious, but as weak
As any babe, and his unceasing cry
Is ' Let my mother come before I die !' "

And the two parents, by his tone bereft
    Well-nigh of hope, passed to the sick man's side ;
While Ella in her loneliness was left
    Waiting without, uncalled. Should Death divide
Their hearts for ever, leaving still the cleft
    Between his soul and hers unbridged and wide?
She lingered ; oft against her will she heard
The tender sighing of a farewell word.

Was there for *her* no longing and no call,
    Not even one poor good-bye message, sent
Like ears of corn that careless hands let fall
    For one who gleans—was this her punishment?
Was parting not enough, without the gall
    Of this immedicable pain, unblent
With joy, and stinging backward, till at last
It should empoison all the sacred Past?

But now the two came out to her ; their tears
    Were dried, and in their faces there was calm ;
The father seemed as one who dimly hears
    The music of some new revealing psalm ;
The mother, past all hopes and past all fears
    And memories of anger, with cold palm
Pressed Ella's hand—" Go in," she said, " be brave,
He loves you now—yes, even to the grave."

He loved her—then the utmost bitterness
    Was gone from pain, leaving remembered joy
Unsullied—happy they who still possess
    Gladness in grief embalmed, that cannot cloy
With full fruition, nor by time grow less,
    Nor can estrangement any more destroy
This Love ideal : thus doth Heaven accord
Through Death, its one immutable reward.

She went in softly ; he lay white and still,
    Though his dark eyes unquenched were burning clear ;
She laid her hand in his, already chill,
    And heard his faint voice whisper, " Dear, more dear
In death—forgive me, Ella, and fulfil
    My last petition, for the end is near,
Is close ; oh stay, and hold awhile my hand,
And listen—only *you* will understand.

"Stay with me, while I linger on the verge
    Of the unknown abyss, yet void of awe
And fear, and ecstasy ; I hear a dirge
    Wailing that Vision which of old I saw ;
Yet not in darkness but in glory merge
    My dreams, and yield to some transcendent Law,
I know not how ; for all is plunged and drowned
In the bright waters of this peace profound.

" But that my eyesight wanes, now might I see ;
　　But that my thoughts grow dim, at last might learn ;
But that sleep weighs me down so wearily,
　　Rise to that Truth, for whose pure light I yearn :
Unworshipped on her mount she dwells, in free
　　And maiden loneliness ; her wooers turn
Toward fair reflected images, that gleam
And waver with the mist or with the stream.

" I cannot think, and scarcely can I feel—
　　But you are strong, and now again you shine
Truth's radiant herald, come to wound and heal
　　A generation hungry for a sign—
Be no sign granted, saving to unseal
　　The meaning of the ages, and unshrine
All errors, all illusions—theirs, my own :
For though the wine-press that I trod alone

" Held blood-red grapes from the volcano's edge,
　　Yet the true purple full-ripe fruit I missed :
Seek you and find ; oh give this one last pledge—
　　Ella, my Love—my Wife !"　His lips she kissed
With tender lingering pressure : sacrilege
　　It seemed, to mar that silent Eucharist
By uttered vow ; the very soul of each
Shone visible, disrobed of veiling speech.

Grieve not for them ; but rather grieve for such
　　As live with what they love, and night and noon
Have joy of gentle voice and kindly touch,
　　Yet famish for some unimagined boon ;
Too little Heaven they have, and all too much
　　Of Earth, whose bounties deaden, late or soon,
Their aspiration ; or its torrent-force
Frays out some fleshly or ethereal course.

For such your grief ; what husbands and their wives
　　Once in long years each other's soul can see ?
But these found all to which high Passion strives—
　　Perfect communion, from cold symbols free,
The fleeting quintessence of myriad lives,
　　A concentrated brief Eternity,
The mountain-vista of an endless age
Not known by weary winding pilgrimage.

At length she spoke—" Myself I dedicate
　　To this great service : all my spirit's power—
Through joy and grief, in good or evil fate,
　　Whether the desert pathways bud and flower,
Or the fair fields be ravaged by man's hate—
　　Shall bear the superscription of this hour :
I give whate'er I have of strength and skill ;
Trust me in this—what Woman can, I will."

Then she was silent : for his look was fraught
  With peace that quenches all desire and dread.
Yet spares the impress of each noble thought
  That ruled in life the converse of the dead :
As Night brings every trivial thing to nought,
  While still the mountains tower, the oceans spread :
Long time she knelt ; and when at last she rose
Her features almost mirrored his repose.

THE ELIXIR OF LIFE.

THE ELIXIR OF LIFE

I.

In some strange waking vision I beheld
   A man and woman in their summer prime,
Who seemed memorial forms of classic eld,
   And yet the fairest, newest births of Time ;
My heart they rapt, my questionings they quelled :
   But now I bid my plain ungilded rhyme
Repeat the marvels that I saw and heard
Vivid in colour and distinct in word.

The man was such as Grecian sculptors took
   For model of a god ; he well might cope
With any deity who ever shook
   The lance or lyre ; he seemed incarnate Hope :
And there was joyous foresight in his look,
   As though the Present were a telescope
Through which appeared the Future's nebulous haze
Clear sky, with constellated suns ablaze.

Yet, gazing in his dark unfathomed eyes,
　　You might behold long mournful ages pass,
Each laying down a load of mysteries
　　Solved by his mind ; you saw, as in a glass,
Your own thoughts and the world's thoughts, mad or wise,
　　Fleet, ever adding to the winnowed mass ;
As though Apollo, King of laughing Hours,
With Time's old scythe should reap the grass and flowers.

Tall was the woman ; beautiful and lithe,
　　Filled full of life in eye, and lip, and hair,
Whose coils like dull-gold serpents seemed to writhe
　　About her royal forehead broad and fair ;
Her sapphire eyes were bright, their glance was blithe,
　　Yet if you caught it sideways, unaware,
Now and again, behind the lustre glad
Floated a shade, half cynic and half sad.

One moment she would seem an angel, fresh
　　From Heaven, and bringing joyful news to man :
The next, a shuddering hint of World and Flesh
　　And Devil, swiftly through your senses ran ;
But then her eyes and voice would quite enmesh
　　Your soul, and you could neither bless nor ban—
Happy, if ere the Siren's isle you passed
Your Fate had lashed you safely to the mast !

Together in a frescoed hall they sate,
  Storied with pictures fair of many lands :
Old Rome, and sad Palmyra desolate,
  And Alpine summits, and Arabian sands ;
Fair ladies rode with knights inamorate,
  And little children played in merry bands ;
But not a group so bright was painted there
That it might shadow forth the living pair.

He held her hand, yet seemed to wander through
  Long years of thought ; till she the silence broke,
And made of her soft voice a silken clue
  To guide him back ; these gentle words she spoke—
" Dearest, this day you promised to endue
  My heart with mirth celestial, and evoke
Visions of joy, whose glories should prevail
O'er all the marvels of Arabian tale."

Light was her tone ; but he, with accent grave,
  Said—" Hear me, Marah ! In my power I keep
A boon more precious than you hope or crave,
  Or even dream in waking or in sleep ;
Such bridal gift as no man ever gave
  To his fair Empress ; a delight as deep
E'en as our love, which ne'er shall fade and flee
Like pallid loves of weak mortality.

S

" Nay, start not, shrink not !   Ages have gone by
    Since in a slumbrous German town I dwelt,
And from my jutting gable saw the sky
    Narrowed but clear ; there did my childhood melt
In fires of youth ; and every day more high
    Ran my life's rushing stream, until I felt
That never must chill Death the torrent freeze,
But it must spread and foam in boundless seas.

" Life, dear Life, human Life ! for this I prayed—
    To be a goblet filled up to the brim
With Life's rich wine ; not an ethereal shade,
    A naked spirit passionless and dim,
But perfect Man, imperishably made,
    With Immortality in heart and limb,
And brain whose orbèd empire might suffice
To hold the World and make it Paradise.

" Thus hoping, searching, in alchemic toil
    I spent the hours of my poor mortal day,
Till Time took youth and vigour as a spoil,
    And bent my frame, and made my temples grey :
Yet still I watched my costly potions boil,
    And with strange herbs and metals did assay
To win, and ever hold in bridal clasp
The Life that flitting mocked my palsied grasp.

" But daily farther from the goal I swerved ;
   Sight left my eyes, and skill my fingers lean :
' Sweet Life '—I cried—' for whom I long have served,
   Whose glorious beauty I from far have seen,
Not such reward thy votary deserved,
   Not this thy warrior's guerdon should have been—
At last, at last, thy full fruition give,
Let me not die, ere I have learned to live !

" ' Yet if thy renovating touch divine
   Too late, too late, be laid on these grey hairs,
I conquer still, though strength should not be mine
   To drink the cup my dying hand prepares ;
Myself, but not my triumph, I resign,
   For all mankind shall be my deathless heirs :
I, friendless, childless, poor, will yet bequeathe
One boon—Eternity for all who breathe !'

" That night, with aching eyes and weary brain,
   Over a seething flask I sadly hung,
And the last precious drops that I could strain
   From my necessities, therein I flung,
Half-fearing 'twere a senile fancy vain
   That one so worn and wrinkled could grow young :
Suddenly, strangely, the thick wizard-broth
Foamed upward in my face with amber froth.

"It fell—and bright the liquid grew and pure
    Like molten topaz ; and a perfume rose
Whose sweetness might a Moslem saint allure
    To drink damnation with his Prophet's foes :
Scarce could my soul this lightning-hope endure,
    My knees were fain to yield, my eyes to close :
I stretched a hand, blind-groping, as I sank
Gasping for breath, and reached the flask, and drank.

"A miracle ! my sight, but now half-quenched,
    Pierced through the gloom, and made the lamplight
        clear ;
I felt my forehead, with deep cares entrenched,
    Grow smooth, and many a sorrow-laden year
Roll like a mist away ; the limbs that blenched
    Were buoyant, and the heart that quaked with fear
Now sang exultantly, in youth renewed,
And strength to bear its own beatitude.

"I dashed the flask to earth with joyous hand—
    'Life, human Life, these drops to thee !' I cried :
I ran and leaped ; I felt my soul expand
    Till all its pettier hopes were glorified
To a great longing that the Earth should stand
    Arrayed in Immortality, a bride,
Wedded to Heaven, not as a beggar-wife,
But bringing her own dower of boundless life.

" And those bright drops that on the floor I threw
    In the exuberant lavishness of health
Brought forth, by magic of their golden dew,
    All tints, and shapes, and substances of wealth ;
A glorious sculptured palace round me grew,
    Whose mystic builders wrought unseen, by stealth ;
Frescoes there were and statues, gold and gems,
And sceptres, and Imperial diadems.

" Yet all these marvels were but promises
    And gracious foretastes of a world unknown ;
I must go forth, a happier Heracles,
    With hydra-headed Death to strive alone,
Fill with new wine all poisoned chalices,
    Anoint all wounds ; revengeful Time dethrone,
Crowning and sceptring in his stead at last
A perfect Present, that should ne'er be Past.

" I sought the mother-land of many hopes—
    Land of the sun, whose summer rays illume
Blue lakes, engarlanded by golden slopes,
    And valleys dim with amethystine bloom ;
The wondrous land of scholars, painters, Popes,
    The Church's cradle, and the Empire's tomb :
Dear land, my promised Canaan of delights,
Peopled, alas, by soft-tongued Canaanites.

" I knew fair Florence in her noon-day glow,
  And in her late repentance and remorse ;
Saw the first joy of Michel Angelo
  When great Lorenzo marked his budding force,
And pacing at Careggi to and fro
  Heard silver-voiced Mirandola discourse,
Though from San Marco thrilled a note of fear—
' Repent, repent ! the sword of God is here !'

" And then I entered those Imperial walls
  Where every epoch finds its magnet-pole,
And watched the great Cathedral's doméd halls
  Rise, and Life's yellow Tiber-current roll,
And heard wise Leo and his Cardinals
  Wittily prate of God and of the Soul,
Or lightly mock, as Teuton ravings drunk,
The thundering theses of the rebel monk.

" But I beheld a black abyss of lust
  And hatred yawn beneath Italia's prime—
Groaning I said, ' Where is a man so just,
  So wise, that he should live beyond his time ?
What poet, priest, or woman can I trust
  To use in righteousness my gift sublime ?
Or shall I aid the crude one-sided plan
Of friar Augustine or Dominican ?'

" And so I kept my boon, and sought anew
   For one to share it.   Now in tranquil seas
I coasted, where they lap with waters blue
   The white or ruddy sands ; with westward breeze
I sailed, that proud Iberian land to view
   Made Empress by the ill-starred Genoese,
Fain to rule Europe, as she ruled her slaves
In diamond mines beyond Atlantic waves.

" But here, 'mid wealth and courtesy and pride
   Methought the vale of Hinnom ever burned,
There tender maids and youths in torture died,
   Parents and children, sages, hinds unlearned,
Who all with blind heroic faith defied
   Faith blindly tyrannous ; heartsore I turned
From the grim King, who seemed what proverbs tell
Of his Madrid—' half winter and half hell.'

" Now to the valiant island, which that King
   Had thought to win with mightiest armament :
There gladsomely I heard at heaven's gate sing
   Blithe birds of morn ; and though the song was blent
With notes unworthy so divine a spring,
   A thrill of joy through all my frame it sent :
But not in city or in court I stayed,
Nor joined the wooers of the Royal Maid.

" It was a midland village that I sought,
    Where daisy-banked a placid river ran
Past a grey church, and near it dwelt and wrought
    A bard whose god-like eyes the heart could scan,
Telling its dreams and humours : but I thought—
    ' Nay, let the Poet live, and leave the Man
To die in peace ; he quaffs his own rich wine
Of Immortality—what needs he mine ?'

" Again I roamed ; in European wars
    I strove, and saw the great Gustavus fall,
In the red carnage that my soul abhors
    Mingled, that I might know and suffer all,
Warring, with vanquished or with conquerors,
    O'er burning home and shattered city-wall,
Till peace returned—then, tired in heart and hand,
I sought the visions of the Morning Land.

" And first I pilgrimed to the Holy Grave
    Where fought of old the flower of Europe's might—
For the benignant Prince of Peace, who gave
    Not peace, but sword and fire, long raged the fight :
There now divided Christians scowl and rave,
    Armenian, Latin, Greek, and Maronite :
Loathing I left them ; then o'er sand and foam
Passed to an elder worship's dreamful home.

"Often at night I heard the lion's roaring
  From the wild jungles of some pathless wood ;
I saw the zonëd Himalayas soaring
  To Arctic heights ; and sought a brotherhood
Not found in age-long roving and exploring,
  Among the saints of Brahma and of Buddh :
But no fit sharer of a lofty fate
Rose from that primal race degenerate.

"Two human lifetimes, alien from the West
  I roved ; then turning, found all Europe lit
With war—with strange convulsions sore distressed ;
  And that fair feminine city of keen wit
Which made of Earth and Heaven a graceful jest
  Read her own doom in ruddy lightnings writ—
'Summed, weighed, found wanting, rent :' her King was
      slain,
Her Queen, her nobles, that the crushed might reign.

"It was the hey-day of that cursëd spawn
  Of rebels, bred and schooled by Tyranny,
That dyed them through and through, and now withdrawn
  Left them indeed unsovereigned, but not free :
And yet it was the drear and blood-red dawn
  Of a new hope for sad Humanity :
I watched a fresh enthusiasm's birth,
Not for high Heaven, but for the suffering Earth.

" I knew the man who touched the secret nerve
　　Of Gallic life, and thrilled it as he would ;
One of those meteor-minds, which never swerve,
　　But dash straight down to their selected good,
Not orbing in a planet's constant curve,
　　Nor comet-soaring through infinitude,
But flashing for a moment, earthward hurled,
The iron fragment of some starry world.

" Then sailed I West, to that Republic free
　　Which bravely to old Britain bade defiance ;
I saw how Christians fostered slavery,
　　How Freedom with Corruption made alliance ;
And thence returned, to give unrestingly
　　One life to Metaphysics, one to Science,
And one to Politics, that I might know
The varied springs of human weal and woe.

" Now am I made the King of this fair State,
　　Which I will rule as mortal man rules not ;
My gathered wisdom will I dedicate
　　To general concord, of just laws begot ;
Then Paradise shall blossom new-create,
　　Not marred by any fraudful serpent-plot,
And Truth and Right the human soul uplift,
Till men be worthy of my glorious gift.

"While still I roamed, my heart I shut and sealed
    Against all passionate love ; yet oftentimes
When dark Italian orbs their light revealed,
    Or the blue eyes besung in Northern rhymes
Glanced coyly, almost would my spirit yield ;
    As though the sure-foot mountaineer who climbs
Some Alpine crag, should loiter on the brink
To pluck the gentian or the mountain pink.

" But in a myriad women, none I found
    So filled and flushed with Life's exuberant tide
That through uncounted ages it could bound
    And ne'er grow stagnant, weak, or satisfied ;
No joy so rich and vital, that undrowned
    On the broad flood in triumph it could ride :
How should a fragile creature, fashioned fair
For her brief hour, my endless being share ?

" But now I have my kingdom and have you
    Gloriously framed for an immortal fate,
Almost that regal beauty might subdue
    Grim Death, and his predestined hour undate :
Sing and exult ! for we the World make new,
    Our dual Star all trancëd hopes await ;
The Future is our own—who will may claim
The unregretted Past, of deathful fame.

" And you to-night, this very night, shall drink
    Immortal Life."   He ceased, and fixed on her
That look, where all the æons seemed to sink
    In one bright Now ; but did my senses err,
Or did I see her for an instant shrink
    Before she answered, " Dearest harbinger
Of gladness !" with a smile so softly bright
That I believed it in my own despite.

THE Vision changed.   And now I saw the Queen
　　In a fair garden loiter ; at her side
Was one of stalwart frame and princely mien,
　　His dark eyes bright with passion and with pride,
Yet not her lord.   They reached an arbour green,
　　Blossomed with roses, and o'er-canopied
With bowering trees ; nor marked amid the shade
A slim shape rustle, like a Dryad-maid.

Marah was speaking, "'Tis a wondrous tale !
　　He has the true Elixir—deems me fit
To share it.   Marvel not that I am pale !
　　Oh weary fancy, nevermore to quit
His side, but while the ages drag and trail
　　In his Elysian theatre to sit,
Or act in dramas classic and sublime
Until I almost long for pantomime !

" I could have loved him ; but he is a god,
    And I am not a goddess or a saint ;
For twenty generations he has trod
    This evil earth, seeing through rags and paint
To its vile heart ; and now he bids me plod
    With him for slow millennia : sooth, 'tis quaint
That *I* am chosen by this clear-eyed sage
His Empress, and ensample to the Age !

" I'd worship him, if he were carved in marble,
    And every morning I could come and kneel
Before his sacred shrine, and softly warble
    The shivering adoration that I feel,
Nor need his philanthropic Law to garble
    With any gloss of selfish woe or weal ;
Then could I yield, like pious Christians many,
The pound to Cæsar, and to God the penny.

" At first, indeed, 'twas sweet and wonderful
    To feel my spirit floating, cradled soft
As on some eagle's wings, who left the dull,
    Stale, petty world, and as he soared aloft
Seemed all my meaner longings to annul ;
    But after journeying sunward long and oft
I hunger and grow faint ; the naked glare
Is too intense, the atmosphere too rare.

" I have not sinned—not yet—but I am weary
    Of all the glories of these ether-flights ;
I'm tired of listening to the concert sphery,
    Dizzy with gazing from Olympian heights :
Dear mortal planet, unideal, cheery,
    Oh give me back thy motley-hued delights—
Give me, for solemn-chanting sun and moon,
A gas-lit ball-room, and a lilting tune !

" I love my life ; and yet a Life Eternal
    Is something far too serious and too vast :
'Twere well, I own, to keep one's beauty vernal,
    But even vanity might pall at last ;
Better to tempt at once the Powers Infernal
    Than with an ever-young enthusiast
Live for Humanity, its evils probe,
And, like old Atlas, hoist the ponderous globe.

" But he will test me—find me out some day,
    And know with what delusive light I shone ;
Then will he bid me in his lordly way
    With just a touch of sorrow—' Hence —begone !'
Or else will strip the gauzy wings so gay
    From his poor worthless weak ephemeron :
Cruel it were, the fire-fly's life to mar,
Because it is an insect, not a star !

" Hear me, good Hubert ! yet you are not good—
    He is a whole infinitude above
Your noblest ; I were happy, if I could
    Cleave to him, wed his thought, his virtues prove :
Were I the archetype of womanhood
    As he of manhood, then we two might love ;
Then should I deem your passion, at the best,
But a dull fable, or a sorry jest.

"Nay, Hubert, do not frown !   I like you well ;
    I am a woman of the world, you know,
Too tired by far to rave about the spell
    Of mutual love, and tremblingly to glow
With girlish raptures ; but to you I tell
    My thoughts and wishes, be they high or low-
That frown again—oh free me from this bond,
Then shall you find me sweet, caressing, fond !

" Oh set me free ! bear me away, away,
    To cold Kamschatka or to burning Ind—
If you should shrink or fail, I needs must pray
    Some ocean current or some rushing wind
To take me—I am mean, and must obey
    My own mean heart ; the boast, ' I have not sinned,'
Was vain ; for sinned I have in wish and thought
Cares Conscience in what stuff the sin is wrought ?"

He clasped her close.   " Fair Queen of my desire,
   Flower of all loveliness ! I do your will
Because it is my own, with heart on fire—
   But from the plan is one thing lacking still ;
For *we* two, sweetest Marah, could not tire,
   And in millennia could not take our fill
Of joyance—we should gaily revel on,
And wondering cry—' Another cycle gone !'

"Short life is all a mocking game of chance ;
   Years are the counters—one by one we lose
And soon grow bankrupt—lucky Circumstance
   Comes late, and we its blandishments refuse
Because we are too old to sing or dance,
   Love we forget, and wealth we cannot use :
Man stakes his all upon a single cast—
Give him a myriad, and he wins at last.

" Then let us of that magic wine partake
   This night, and fathom all the depths of pleasure,
And live without satiety or ache
   Our feastful days, that Time forgets to measure :
How shall we cheat this chemist-King, and make
   Ourselves possessors of his liquid treasure ?
His servants love him ; vainly should we try
With stores of gold the loyal fools to buy.

                            T

" But I will give you a prepotent draught
    To set before your deathless lord to-night,
Saying—' Come, pledge me ! not till you have quaffed
    This cup, I taste of your Elixir's might !'
So shall we capture life and love by craft,
    For as he drinks, he will be reft of sight,
Hearing, and thought, by slumber—you are free !
Then quick ! the goblet seize, and haste to me

" That we may drink deep, deep, of boundless bliss "—
    But she—" It is not poison ?" faintly asked—
" To poison he is mortal—spare me this !"
    Lord Hubert turned aside ; the fiend unmasked
Glared from his face ; but soon with tender kiss
    Again his power of smooth deceit he tasked,
Saying—" This potion does not harm, but cures—
I would not hurt a hound that had been yours !"

The foliage shook ; they saw a light shape spring,
    And toward the palace dart.   " We are betrayed,"
Cried Marah, " hastes she not to warn the King ?
    Prate, ready tongue !—a ready hand had stayed
Her flight.   I know her—heard her carolling
    That foolish story of the beggar-maid
And King Cophetua, long ere I was doomed
To life, and in immortal love entombed."

Leaving the guilty pair in their dismay,
   My dream pursued the maiden's flying feet ;
Fragile she was, and slender as a fay,
   Fair streamed her tresses as she glided fleet,
Her white robe flashed—she sped with no delay
   Till at the gate I heard her voice entreat
That she might see her sovereign, kind to grant
The prayers of many a humble suppliant.

They led her where he sate ; then, cowering low,
   She said—" My liege, I oft have made your sport—
You know me not, perchance—how should you know
   A simple singing-maiden of your court ?
I would not seek you for my private woe,
   But I have that to tell which would extort
Language, though I were dumb, and give me breath
For warning speech, though cold I lay in death."

She faltered—then at once she oped the sluice
   Of words and tears, and told the plot accurst,
Adding at last, in weeping self-excuse—
   " I had not stayed to listen, but the first
Word of the Queen foreshadowed some abuse
   Of your deep love—must I not learn the worst,
And fly to save my monarch from the snare ?
Trust me, oh King ! I have no other prayer."

But he abashed her with a searching look—
  "You have an honest face," he said, " but sure
A most deceiving fancy ; you mistook
  Faces or meanings. Nay ! I am secure—
Go, foolish damsel, to your singing-book !
  Hubert I trust not, but the Queen is pure—
Pure as the radiant ether. She shall come
And speak her innocence, and strike you dumb."

He said and smiled ; then to the Queen he sent
  Praying her presence.   Marah came, with lips
Pale but firm-set, and haughty eyes that meant
  To look unchanged on glory or eclipse ;
But when she saw her lord, that bold intent
  Slipped from her, like the outworn slough that slips
From a snake's body ; and forgetting pride
She fell before him.   " I have sinned," she cried,

" And am not worthy to be called your wife—
  No, nor your slave !   That coward in will and deed,
Whose false lips bade me steal your cup of life,
  Has fled, and basely left me at my need,
A double traitor.   Let the vengeful knife
  End my despair—nay, rather will I plead
That you, so merciful, will grant me time
For penitence—perchance forgive my crime

"At last, and—dare I think it ?—in the end
 Take back the woman whom you justly spurned,
To be—ah, not your wife—but yet your friend,
 Long hence, when all my follies are unlearned :
Oh, by the love you bore me, hear and bend,
 And pardon !"   But from that fair form he turned
As from some loathly creature misbegot—
Crying—"Nay, woman ! of my love speak not—

"What I loved *is* not, and has never been ;
 It dies where it was born—in my own heart ;
Yours are the form, the features, and the mien,
 As Hell may hold a seraph's counterpart :
But I reproach you not ; I should have seen,
 I should have better known the Siren's art :
Shall not the sage Physician's blame be mute
When *he* has pressed for wine the poison-fruit ?

"You were to me a light, illusive ghost,
 Not living flesh : as though a man should find
Some portrait fair, and foolishly should boast
 That he in eyes and lips can read the mind,
And know the heart's recesses innermost,
 And so should give himself with passion blind
To a mere phantom—worshipping perchance
The painter's flattery of a harlot's glance.

" You loved your life—the life you understood :
    No man but prizes that which he may call
His life, and lightly names that primal good
    In common phrase, and symbols read by all,
Yet new translated by each alien mood :
    The freeman speaks one language with the thrall,
And yet the simplest words of love and hate,
Passing from one to other, shed their freight.

" Calm is my speech, because my heart is cold,
    Cold, cold, by you fast frozen.   Go your way—
For when that luring fairness I behold,
    And hear the voice, well-loved but yesterday,
I feel as when I grew infirm and old,
    And Life fled from me with a mocking Nay :
Go, Marah—soul and body you bereave
Of youth, and only Age's heart-ache leave."

" Marah !"   She seemed to shudder at the name ;
    Perchance some tardy touch of penitence
Or late-awakening love had stirred her frame,
    Deep-thrilling till it pricked the inward sense :
Trembling she rose, and hung her head in shame
    As though her beauty mirrored her offence ;
Then forth she went, with slow, uncertain pace,
And hands that strove to hide her drooping face.

Now the pale singing-maiden dared to draw
　Near to the King, till at his feet she knelt,
But silently she gazed, held back by awe
　From murmuring or from chanting what she felt ;
And when the timid, upturned look he saw
　Gently he spoke—" Fear not—for you have dealt
Wisely and loyally ; you shall not lose
Your recompense." But she replied—" I choose

" No thanks, or else an infinite reward—
　Make me immortal ! not that life is sweet,
But should your grace this sovereign boon accord
　I may learn wisdom, sitting at your feet ;
Till haply, in a myriad years, my Lord
　Might deem me worthy—but it is not meet
To babble thus." That shame was in her cheeks,
Which, striving to be secret, plainlier speaks.

He laid a pitying hand upon her head—
　" Peace, gentle child ! You know not what you seek ;
Calm is the grave, and restful are the dead,
　But Life is rude, and tempest-tost, and bleak,
And you will tire ere threescore years have sped :
　Your nature is too womanly and weak
To drink my cup, or watch one age with me
In the World's garden of Gethsemane."

Then she too stole away, and he was left
    In darkness and alone.   I thought he strove
To disentangle all the ravelled weft
    Of wrath and weariness, and scorn and love ;
At first like the unquiet shade, long reft
    Of hope, who paces some Tartarean grove :
But when he spoke, his voice, though sad, untuned,
Told not of an immedicable wound.

" Marah ! with mind that might have soared beyond
    The highest Heaven of woman, yet was bent
Even to Hell ! was it for you I conned
    The World—an age to every lineament ?
If I were mortal, now must I despond,
    Or from despair step downward to content :
But he whose portion is perpetual youth
May watch and fail, and still have time for Truth.

" Love shrivels to black dust, but leaves alive
    Duty and Hope.   When not a flower remains
Unblighted, still the leafy boughs survive,
    And still the sap is mounting in their veins ;
No more, no more, my lonely life shall strive
    To put forth blossoms, nurturing canker-stains ;
Yet shall the tree aspire, and gather might
By broader foliage from a clearer light.

" Too late, too late ! such dolorous cry was mine,
　　Such words my doubting spirit sighed of yore ;
They are the brand of death—the fatal sign
　　Proving wise man, with all his dear-bought lore
Of evil and of good, not yet divine :
　　' Too late, too late !' I know the words no more—
' Live and prevail !' is written in their stead,
In golden letters for their sanguined red.

" Death, living death ! thou canst not bid me grieve
　　Eternally, because a woman's lip
Was beautiful and cunning to deceive :
　　Now, since nor love is mine nor fellowship,
More gloriously my life I will enweave
　　With general gladness, and for ever strip
My soul of passion ; even as the Sun
Lavishes glowing heat, but garners none.

" All private hope is frail and fugitive,
　　Dead if it miss or if it reach its goal ;
There is one way of peace, but one—to live
　　The universal Life ; to make the whole
Of Nature mine ; to feel the laws which give
　　Form to her Being, sovereign in my soul :
By this one road, enfranchisement I gain
From the heart-stifling narrowness of pain.

" Thus I exalt this anguish finely-nerved
  To poignant thought and aspiration keen :
Oh Life, stern Life, for whom in woe I served,
  Whose veilëd beauty I so long have seen,
If such reward thy votary deserved,
  If this thy warrior's guerdon should have been,
At last, at last, be perfect bounty shown,
And all thy pulses vibrate in my own !

" Come to me, come to me, from sea and star !
  From all thy homes, from all thy fountains, come !
Oh let me feel thy throbbings near and far,
  And give full utterance to thy voices dumb :
Make me thy true, thy radiant Avatar,
  And in my action concentrate the sum
Of thy unseen endeavours ; let its plan
Image the secret destiny of Man.

" Surely thy end and meaning is not loss,
  Surely thou workest to some joy untold ;
Some Book of Life there is, not writ across
  With runes of woe and dirges manifold ;
Some fire thou hast, to purge away the dross
  Of Death, deep grainëd in thy purest gold :
From all things save the quintessence of Thee—
From Hate, from Love—oh Life, deliver me !"

Then was he silent ; in that human breast
    Immortal, sorrow seemed at war with thought ;
The tears burst forth : like the empoisoned vest
    Of Jove-born Heracles, remembrance wrought :
Fainter, more distant, grew the murmurs pressed
    From that heroic heart ; my Vision, fraught
With marvels, faded, and a chilly stream
Of work-day light poured in and quenched the dream.

THE STORY OF CLARICE.

THE STORY OF CLARICE.

I.

In an old house, wind-haunted, bare, and grim,
    Fair Clarice and her father lived alone
With books for comrades ; books were slaves to him
    But friends to her ; among them she had grown
For well-nigh twenty summers ; though the sage
Who gave her being, scarcely knew her age.

Like a wise pedlar, vending where he can
    A ribbon, a gilt pin, a crystal bead,
That yellow, smoke-dried, literary man
    Wrote books that all might quote, though none would
        read :
He raked the dust-heaps of the Court of France,
And left his daughter to herself—and Chance.

But she, in virgin majesty serene,
    Whom few had dared to love, and none to woo,
Wore learning as a long-descended queen
    Her robes and crown doth royally endue ;
As though what others con with aching head
This maiden knew by right inherited.

Stately, with clear grey eyes and flaxen hair,
    She might have seemed Athene, wise and chaste,
Save that no lofty helmet she did wear,
    Nor ægis buckled to her slender waist ;
Nor could she teach what worldly snares to shun,
As the great Goddess taught Ulysses' son.

Grave was her mouth, and yet was formed for smiles ;
    Pale were her cheeks—how lovely, had they blushed !
No sweet gay looks were hers, no girlish wiles :
    Not that her woman's instincts had been crushed ;
But, like azaleas in a darkened room,
They had not air and light enough to bloom.

I said the maid was left to Chance—'tis true—
    But that Divinity has divers shapes ;
Now, she appears an apple rich of hue,
    Eve's fruit or Discord's—now, the juice of grapes,
Promising mirth—now, a fair human form,
With tender words, and sighs, and love-looks warm.

She came to Clarice as a scholar young,
    The secretary of her pedant sire ;
Gentle of mien and eloquent of tongue
    He spoke with something of a poet's fire :
Well might accomplished Wilfred hope to gain
The maiden's guileless heart and book-learn'd brain.

His mind was all o'ergrown with metaphor,
    With tropes that simulate and stifle thought ;
Right glibly could he wage a wordy war,
    Skilled in debate, not lightly tripped or caught :
Yet oft with her he faltered and grew hoarse,
And lost the gilded thread of his discourse.

His face—in sooth, it was a handsome face,
    Quick to express whate'er he dreamed or felt ;
His dark eyes glowed with all-subduing grace,
    Sure of their power to brighten, kindle, melt :
Yet Wilfred's practised heart poor Clarice stole,
And reigned unconscious tyrant of his soul.

For, spite of all her wisdom, she was still
    So calm, so child-like, and so marble-cold,
She did not know he loved her, nor had skill
    To read in looks what no sweet words had told :
Though tales of love her spirit oft could reach
Like distant warblings in a foreign speech.

She knew the woes of Dido ; she could tell
    How Helen set the towers of Troy ablaze :
She thought of Love as a forgotten spell,
    Potent in far-off lands, in ancient days ;
Obsolete now, like Magic black and white,
Or the Emission Theory of Light.

U

But once she prayed the youth, his day s work done,
    To read, and she would listen : with fresh hopes
He took the philosophic malison
    Of Schopenhauer, king of misanthropes,
And chose the chapter where a sunny mist
Floats o'er the pages of the Pessimist.

For there, in mildest mood, he tells how Art
    Reveals the pure Idea, soothes desire,
Sets free the mind, and heals the aching heart ;
    But chief he vaunts the magic of the lyre—
Sweet peace and tranquil ecstasy it gives,
And breathes the inmost life of all that lives.

So rapt was queenly Clarice, so intent
    On Wilfred's voice, he could not meet her look ;
Its very chillness fired him—on he went,
    Halting and stammering—then flung down the book
And spoke and gazed as every man, not dunce
Or icicle, has gazed and spoken once.

" Too long have I stood blindfold on the brink
    Of Heaven or Hell ; and now I dare at length
To pray for sight—I scarce can speak or think
    Because with all my soul and all my strength
And all my life I love you—Clarice, hear !"
And his voice quivered with a passionate fear.

Oh gentle heart that could not understand !
   Oh cruel calm in wondering childlike eyes !
She let him clasp her unresponsive hand,
   And froze him with her innocent surprise—
Then plucked her hand away, cut short his prayer,
Fled from the room, and left him planted there.

Blankly he stood ; one miserable course
   Alone remained—to take his hat, and go—
Though still he kept the lover's sad resource,
   To rail on the cold heart that made his woe,
And switch with savage cane the wayside flower,
And curse himself, and Fate, and Schopenhauer.

II.

Clarice awoke next morning with the sense
   That something she had found, and something lost ;
A little pain she felt, but knew not whence,
   A little loosening of her vestal frost :
And she was sad for *him*—not knowing yet
How lightly men can love, how soon forget.

'Twas a grey, misty, miserable day,
   And he would sit, she thought, alone and drear
In dingy lodgings ; or perchance would stray
   Out in the busy street, with none to cheer,
No one to sound his lonely heart's abysm,
And comfort him with German Pessimism.

A stirring as of springtide he had wrought
   In that fair breast which yet he could not win :
She pitied, and she wondered, and she thought :
   They say that Pity is to Love akin—
Agreed—with one important reservation—
She is at best a very poor relation.

For Clarice neither loved the swain himself,
   Nor dreamed of being some day some one's wife ;
But he, like those great Germans on the shelf,
   Suggested a new way of viewing life :
The first poor swallow does not make a summer,
Yet is he a thrice memorable comer.

Her father—might she speak to him ? In vain !
   He would have scorned a modern love affair ;
It never entered his most learned brain
   That this unmothered daughter needed care ;
And he was seeking, in that dust-heap dark,
Some mouldy scandal touching Joan of Arc.

She had no comrades ; books were all her friends ;
   And even these had failed her utterly,
For none could teach her how to make amends,
   None could restore her nature's harmony ;
Nor found she any grief so vague as hers
Recorded by the ancient chroniclers.

The classic beauty either loves her wooer,
   Or else she hates him in the same degree :
Daphne was glad to 'scape her bright pursuer
   By branching out into a laurel-tree ;
Queen Dido slew herself that luckless day
When the too pious Trojan sailed away.

These old companions have no kindly aid
    For any heart in lore of love unlearned ;
So, of her fluctuating thoughts afraid,
    To Spenser and to Shakespeare Clarice turned,
And read of all sweet ladies wooed by men,
From Una chaste to wifely Imogen.

She read, and pondered, and read o'er again
    The moonlight vows of glowing Juliet ;
She read how scorning doubt, delay, and pain,
    Sir Scudamour found white-robed Amoret,
And led her by the coy resisting hand
From sovran Cytherea's priestess-band.

And much she marvelled how such things might be ;
    " And such things are," she thought, " this very day,
But Heaven in grace has left me fancy-free,
    And this is well ; and *he* is gone away :
My father now must analyse alone
Those blotches on the shield of valiant Joan."

But, as the days and weeks and months went on,
    Less calm she grew ; more anxious to believe
That she was happier since the youth had gone,
    That she was no fond simple girl, to grieve
For a mere fantasy ; but ne'ertheless
She oft forgot her reasoned happiness.

And having no one else to think about,
  She thought of Wilfred ; seemed to see him, hear
Him speak : and his successor was a lout
  Who made that inward vision doubly clear ;
For slow he was of speech, and dull of eye,
And short, and round, and rubicund, and shy.

In study and in dreams, one long year passed :
  The house seemed shadowed by some direful ban :
For every day was lonelier than the last,
  Each book the dullest ever writ by man :
Clarice had half begun to doubt her boast,
When—a three-volume novel came by post !

She knew the writing—rapid, firm, and fine ;
  She looked within—and there was Wilfred's name—
The letters rose and danced along the line,
  Mocking her quivering lips and cheeks aflame ;
This was his book, his voice, his heart ; she sighed,
And turned the leaves with a sad thrill of pride.

'Twas the first novel she had ever read—
  Think of it, Mudie's votaries and Smith's !
Ambrosially her sky-born soul was fed
  On the sun's poetry in old-world myths,
But never knew what wealth of weed and flower
His tireless beams engender hour by hour.

And Wilfred's heroine was a maiden queen
    Like Clarice, bred on such Olympian food :
Surely she saw her own transfigured mien—
    " But no," she thought, " for I am not so good,
So fair—some other's portrait this must be,
And her he loves, and has forgotten me."

She read with pain and pleasure ; now she pored,
    Jealously, o'er some page with passion fraught,
And wondered what fair Goddess he adored ;
    Now, her heart sprang to meet some bright-clad thought;
For thoughts there were, rich ears of harvest-gold,
Not choked with tares and poppies, as of old.

Not one day thus she pored, but many days ;
    She knew the volumes three almost by heart,
She lived in the book's life, thought in its phrase,
    And so for weeks she conned and mused apart ;
Till, as it chanced, one afternoon there came
A visitor of antiquarian fame.

A blear-eyed bookworm ; yet he was a shade
    More human than her father ; he had penned
Stout vindications of the slandered Maid
    Of Orleans, till he half estranged his friend :
He took the scutcheon of that virgin knight,
And either whitewashed, or else washed it white.

Now the pair sat and argued ; but at last
   The visitor, right glad to end the strife
When Clarice entered, left the angry past,
   And stooped to safer themes of modern life ;
Of dynamite he spoke, and what could ail
The Irish ; then of books—of Wilfred's tale.

" The book is good—or rather, not so bad
   As one might augur from its great success ;
You know the young romancer—it is sad
   When budding brains are doomed to idleness ;
For he is ill—they say, in doubtful case,
Alone, in lodgings,"—and he named the place.

Poor Clarice stole away ; the old man's words
   Chilled her like death ; she saw the sun grow dim,
And like the fluttering of imprisoned birds
   She felt wild pulses throb in every limb :
To a dull corner of her room she crept,
And there, till night was black, she crouched and wept.

But in the midnight watches she began,
   Thinking of *his* pain, to forget her own ;
And all her strenuous soul was bent to plan
   How she might aid him ; for that word—" Alone,"
Rang in her ears ; she knew, as ne'er before,
The load of bitter meaning that it bore.

Pure innocence—what counsellor is worse ?—
  Guided and guarded her in all she did ;
She had no friend, not even an old nurse,
  To tell her what was lawful, what forbid ;
And so resolved—lacking such nurse or friend–
That Wilfred she must seek, and watch, and tend.

Then Clarice slept, and dreamed that Wilfred's book
  Became a world ; its chapters palaces ;
And she its Goddess : but an earthquake shook
  The domes of light and rainbow terraces :
The miraged earth engulphed its phantom race,
And left its two Immortals face to face.

III.

" How lightly men can love, how soon forget !"
　　I said—yet some there be not false or fickle :
For one, the blind god wings an arrowlet
　　No deadlier pointed than a sweetbriar prickle ;
For one, a dart fledged with Tartarean flame,
Barbed, venomed, and thrice cursed in Hecate's name.

Neither the rose-thorn nor the poisoned arrow
　　Was sped for Wilfred—but a keen-tipped shaft,
That rankled deep, yet pierced not bone and marrow,
　　And still he dined, debated, jested, laughed ;
The while his heart was like a tooth, whose fang
Aches with dull woe, or with fierce throbbing pang.

For one bright image lived before his eyes ;
　　Where'er he moved, the haunting shape was there :
And long he pondered what rich sacrifice
　　Could win its beauty ; till the vision fair,
As saint from heaven instructs an eremite,
Taught her sad thrall to worship her aright.

She made herself the centre of a world
　　Peopled with gracious phantoms indistinct ;
But, as he gazed, a golden mist upfurled,
　　And all was clearly shaped, and brightly tinct :
How could he choose but chronicle from far
The story of that new-created star ?

And thus he dreamed and wrote, until his dream
　　Was all set forth in fine-writ manuscript ;
He felt, at the last page of the last ream,
　　As though in some great argosy he shipped
His wealth : not with the trader's avarice keen,
But as the hard-won ransom of a queen.

And the book prospered wheresoe'er it went ;
　　Much fame had Wilfred, and a little gold,
Yet thought of the one copy that he sent
　　To Clarice, more than of the hundreds sold ;
And for her smile, had been content to lose
Even the most nectareous of reviews.

'Tis sweet, in truth, to feel oneself a god
　　Shaping with words a spirit-universe,
Touching to various life the formless clod,
　　Winning fresh glory e'en from Fate perverse,
That foe to plans divine and human toils,
Which like a snake in every Eden coils.

Such deities are mortal ; and when these,
  As once their sire Apollo, love in vain,
And grant the willing mind no hour of ease,
  But still toward high achievement strive and strain,
What marvel if the genial visage pales,
And the pulse languishes, and the strength fails ?

'Twas thus with Wilfred ; though the bookworm old
  Had somewhat overdrawn his piteous plight,
Most truly might that learned man have told
  Of many a torpid day and tossing night,
Filled with sick hope of one approving line
From Clarice—but there came no word or sign.

One cheerless afternoon, upon his couch
  Brooding he lay ; there came a tap - the door
Soft-opened—sure his dazzled eyes could vouch
  That the fair image kept in his heart's core
They saw ; come haply as a cruel wraith,
With cold ethereal gifts to mock his faith.

The maiden entered ; the dim light aslant
  On his pale face, constrained her like a charm :
She felt and seemed a spectral visitant
  Of one in mortal straits ; on languid arm
He raised himself, with an uncertain cry
Of "Clarice!" and sank backward wearily.

Then all the wifehood and the motherhood
　That in her virgin heart close-hidden lay
Sprang forth ; the voice of her quick-pulsing blood
　Rebuked her coming, and yet murmured "Stay !"
She stood there an Olympian goddess mute
And blushing, with soft eyes irresolute.

At last she spoke—" Forgive me ! but I knew
　That you were ill, alone—and I am come
With fruit and medicines—if I weary you,
　Tell me, and bid me go "--here she grew dumb,
And cold, and faint, and all her thoughts forgot,
Because so wild he gazed, yet answered not.

He lay and watched her timid attitudes,
　The rosy colour mantling in her cheek,
Her faltering phrases, with brief interludes
　Of sighs ; he watched, and did not stir or speak :
But when, like one who in strange peril stands,
She tottered, grew death-pale, flung out her hands,

He rose with desperate hunger in his face,
　Clasped her with arms that trembled as they strained,
Kissed the fair head that bent to his embrace,
　The lily cheeks, the eyelids violet-veined ;
And held her long, although she faintly strove
To free herself, in very fear of love.

She did not know the feeling of a kiss,
    Except her father's—which had not been warm—
And now she shrank and shuddered from her bliss
    E'en as a thirsting wretch before the storm
Of wind and rain, that must renew his life,
Unless he die in the tumultuous strife.

At length he half-released her —"Sweet," he said,
    "This is my fruit, my medicine ; were I blind
Now must I see—must live, if I were dead ;
    You are my breath, my pulse, my inmost mind ;
Music you are, whose mournfulness and mirth
Reveal the Will of this phantasmal Earth."

She blushed at his remembrance of that page
    In Schopenhauer—"Ah forgive !" she cried—
" I was a tame-bred goldfinch in its cage,
    Not knowing that the world is all outside ;
Yet such poor birds will beat the bars, and sing
Of hope, and build an idle nest in Spring."

" Yet nay," he smiled, "you are Olympian-born,
    You are Egeria's self, the nymph who blest
Rome's king with laws from Heaven : that gloomy morn
    When I arose from nightmare-laden rest
A banished man, you sent your sprite divine,
That pitying led me to the fountain-shrine."

What more fond vows they uttered—how they planned
   The future's wedded joy—I need not tell,
For every love-taught soul will understand ;
   Nor how, when twilight came, they broke the spell
Reluctantly, that Clarice home might haste,
Yet once again, and still once more embraced.

That night she dreamed that over fertile ground
   And blossomed herbage the two lovers trod ;
The air was filled with an Æolian sound
   That sang of secret life beneath the sod,
And all pure fragrances of flower and fruit
Lived in the music of that fitful lute.

Of couching flocks it chanted ; of the bird
   Nested in shade ; of all things that have breath ;
Of human fate ; and still entranced they heard,
   And knew the harmonies of Birth and Death :
Till downward flowed the dream, and bore her deep
Into the dark unhaunted caves of Sleep.

RESIPISCENTIA, Etc.

RESIPISCENTIA.

" Ye must be born again."

FIRST VOICE.

GOOD morrow, comrade !   Whence that look elate ?
    Where are thy sins and fears, a mocking host ?
One week ago, thou wast as I, who hate
    Both day and night—day most.

SECOND VOICE.

Glad tidings of great joy ! that host is gone !
    I prayed to Christ an unbelieving prayer,
Half blasphemous, half mad—but straight there shone
    Into my soul's despair

A strange, pure light—then on my brow I felt
    A healing hand, and on my sleepless eyes ;
Till, knowing nothing, feeling all, I knelt,
    And with deep groans and sighs

Yielded to Christ my soul, its secret need,
　　Its woe, its doubt, its dread, its self-disdain,
Its myriad petty sins, that grow and breed,
　　And, mob-like, rule the brain.

All these he took away—he made me yield
　　The last regret, the lingering sense of wrong ;
I am as one from year-long tortures healed,
　　Made sound, and hale, and strong—

Who every morning feels a sweet new joy
　　Because he wakes without the accustomed pain :
Who runs and leaps more lightly than a boy,
　　Having been born again

Into a long-forgotten world of health,
　　Where he may woo bright eyes, nor need to fear
That but in pity or in lust of wealth
　　They feign to hold him dear.

Where he with other men may strain and strive—
　　To win he scarcely craves—let it suffice
That heart, brain, limbs, so bounteously alive
　　Are his full Paradise.

Oh come and taste and see what virtues lie
  In this Elixir that has made me whole—
Though thou be sick to death, thou shalt not die—
  Repent, and heal thy soul !

First Voice.

Brave words, my friend—I do not grudge thy mirth ;
  Though life be one remorse, I yet endure,
Well knowing there be ills upon this earth
  Which have not any cure.

Thou hast been lame awhile, and now canst run ;
  Awhile thou hast been blind, but seest now :
Go, leap and praise thy God for strength new-won—
  But I am not as thou.

Pain comes of sudden hurt or slow disease ;
  Break thou a bone, the surgeon sets it well—
But show him leprous sores—will he cure these ?
  Alas, thou canst not tell.

Life as it is, and must be, and has been
    No piecemeal penitence can show aright,
Deeming the one part foul, the other clean,
    Here black, and there snow-white.

That this day week, I left my task unwrought ;
    That yesterday, I said not what I meant ;
That one hour since, I grossly sinned in thought—
    Not thus do I repent.

Nor do I lay a finger on my shame,
    Calling this nerve, that muscle, falsely built ;
I can but say—"This Self, this physical frame,
    Is one incarnate Guilt."

Could I believe thy glorious Gospel true,
    That were no cure for this organic ill :
Can Christ unweave my tissues, mould anew
    The matrix of my will ?

My grief has no beginning and no end ;
    I do repent of antenatal sin,
Whose poisoning juices thread my veins, and blend
    With the fresh life within.

That in my blood this virus I must keep
   To-morrow, next week, next month, all my years,
Until my day of death—for this I weep
   With ignominious tears.

THIRD VOICE.

Nay, hope is thine! Who chants this grim complaint
   Has steadfast heart, free mind, and insight keen ;
Such man may purge away the leprous taint
   While yet he cries " Unclean !"

Daily thy tissues die—are born afresh
   Daily, not moving thee to joy or dole ;
Yet all the slow mutations of thy flesh
   Gently transmute thy soul.

Go, live in hope and labour, fearing nought ;
   Starve the foul germs of hate, and lust, and greed ;
Force day by day thy brain to patient thought,
   Thy hand to earnest deed.

Long were the darkling months before thy birth,
  Long years regenerate a frame defiled :
It may be thou shalt enter heaven on earth
  Clean as a pure-born child.

THE RECLUSE.

" Heu ! Quanto minus est cum reliquis versari, quam tui
meminisse !"

HAVING known Love, all its unmeasured heights,
  All its unfathomed depths, I go my way,
In full content that these supreme delights
  Come not, like meaner pleasures, day by day.

Such lesser joys I yielded with few tears,
  Reserving nought, paying Love's perfect price :
Shall I bewail my thirty desert years,
  I, who have lived three days in Paradise ?

Nay, smile not, friend ! I know not which is best,
  Plucked rosebud, or remembered asphodel,
A mortal wife, or an Olympian guest :
  Well hast thou chosen ; but I, too, chose well.

LOVE'S MIRROR.

I LIVE with love encompassed round,
  And glowing light that is not mine,
    And yet am sad ; for, truth to tell,
    It is not I you love so well ;
Some fair Immortal, robed and crowned,
  You hold within your heart's dear shrine.

Cast out the Goddess ! let me in ;
  Faulty I am, yet all your own,
  But this bright phantom you enthrone
Is such as mortal may not win.

And yet this beauty that you see
  Is like to mine, though nobler far ;
Your radiant guest resembles me
  E'en as the sun is like a star.

Then keep her in your heart of hearts,
  And let me look upon her face,
  And learn of that transcendent grace,
Till all my meaner self departs,

And, while I love you more and more,
  My spirit, gazing on the light,
  Becomes, in loveliness and might,
The glorious Vision you adore.

FRIENDSHIP.

THE human soul that crieth at thy gates,
 Of man or woman, alien or akin,
'Tis thine own Self that for admission waits —
  Rise, let it in.

Bid not thy guest but sojourn and depart;
 Keep him, if so it may be, till the end,
If thou have strength and purity of heart
  To be his friend.

Not only, at bright morn, to wake his mind
 With noble thoughts, and send him forth with
  song,
Nor only, when night falls, his wounds to bind;
  But all day long

To help with love, with labour, and with lore,
 To triumph when, by others' aid, he wins,
To carry all his sorrows, and yet more——
  To bear his sins;

To keep a second conscience in thine own,
   Which suffers wound on wound, yet strongly lives,
Which takes no bribe of tender look or tone,
     And yet forgives.

But, should some mortal vileness blast with death
   Thy love for comrade, leader, kinsman, wife—
Seek no elixir to restore false breath,
     And loathsome life.

Thy love is slain—thou canst not make it whole
   With all thy store of wine, and oil, and bread :
Some passions are but flesh—thine had a soul,
     And that is dead.

CHRIST, THE NAZARENE.

THE copyist group was gathered round
A time-worn fresco, world-renowned,
Whose central glory once had been
The face of Christ, the Nazarene.

And every copyist of the crowd
With his own soul that face endowed,
Gentle, severe, majestic, mean ;
But which was Christ, the Nazarene ?

Then one who watched them made complaint,
And marvelled, saying, " Wherefore paint
Till ye be sure your eyes have seen
The face of Christ, the Nazarene ?"

SONG.

THINK not I roam afield
  With heart untrue ;
The gifts my rambles yield
  Are all for you.

The bird must leave her nest
  And fledglings five,
The honey-bee must rest
  Far from her hive.

New regions I explore
  While day is bright ;
My heart, with richer store,
  Goes home at night.

TIME AND LOVE.

TIME hobbles, but Love flies ;
One moment, say the wise,
   They pass together :
Not Cupid's curls of gold
But Time's grey forelock hold,
   A trusty tether.

For Time, once safely caught,
Is servant to your thought
   For ever after ;
But wanton Love will snip
The curl you hold, and trip
   Away with laughter.

Yet if my hint you heed,
With all his craft and speed,
   He ne'er shall flout you ;
Catch Cupid by the wing,
For then he cannot spring
   To Heaven without you.

EVOLUTIONAL EROTICS

W

SCIENTIFIC WOOING.

I was a youth of studious mind,
Fair Science was my mistress kind,
    And held me with attraction chemic ;
No germs of Love attacked my heart,
Secured as by Pasteurian art
    Against that fatal epidemic.

For when my daily task was o'er
I dreamed of H_2SO_4,
    While stealing through my slumbers placid
Came Iodine, with violet fumes,
And Sulphur, with its yellow blooms,
    And whiffs of Hydrochloric Acid.

My daily visions, thoughts, and schemes
With wildest hope illumed my dreams,
    The daring dreams of trustful twenty :
I might accomplish my desire,
And set the river Thames on fire
    If but Potassium were in plenty !

Alas ! that yearnings so sublime
Should all be blasted in their prime
   By hazel eyes and lips vermilion !
Ye gods ! restore the halcyon days
While yet I walked in Wisdom's ways,
   And knew not Mary Maud Trevylyan !

Yet nay ! the sacrilegious prayer
Was not mine own, oh fairest fair !
   Thee, dear one, will I ever cherish ;
Thy worshipped image shall remain
In the grey thought-cells of my brain
   Until their form and function perish.

Away with books, away with cram
For Intermediate Exam. !
   Away with every college duty !
Though once Agnostic to the core,
A virgin Saint I now adore,
   And swear belief in Love and Beauty.

Yet when I meet her tranquil gaze,
I dare not plead, I dare not praise,
   Like other men with other lasses ;
She's never kind, she's never coy,
She treats me simply as a boy,
   And asks me how I like my classes !

I covet not her golden dower—
Yet surely Love's attractive power
   Directly as the mass must vary—
But ah ! inversely as the square
Of distance ! shall I ever dare
   To cross the gulf, and gain my Mary ?

So chill she seems—and yet she might
Welcome with radiant heat and light
   My courtship, if I once began it ;
For is not e'en the palest star
That gleams so coldly from afar
   A sun to some revolving planet ?

My Mary ! be a solar sphere !
Envy no comet's mad career,
   No arid, airless lunar crescent !
Oh for a spectroscope to show
That in thy gentle eyes doth glow
   Love's vapour, pure and incandescent !

Bright fancy ! can I fail to please
If with similitudes like these
   I lure the maid to sweet communion ?
My suit, with Optics well begun,
By Magnetism shall be won,
   And closed at last in Chemic union !

At this I'll aim, for this I'll toil,
And this I'll reach—I will, by Boyle,
   By Avogadro, and by Davy !
When every science lends a trope
To feed my love, to fire my hope,
   Her maiden pride must cry " *Peccavi !*"

I'll sing a deep Darwinian lay
Of little birds with plumage gay,
   Who solved by courtship Life's enigma ;
I'll teach her how the wild-flowers love,
And why the trembling stamens move,
   And how the anthers kiss the stigma.

Or Mathematically true
With rigorous Logic will I woo,
   And not a word I'll say at random ;
Till urged by Syllogistic stress,
She falter forth a tearful " Yes,"
   A sweet " *Quod erat demonstrandum !*"

THE NEW ORTHODOXY.

So, dear Fred, you're not content
Though I quote the books you lent,
And I've kept that spray you sent
   Of the milk-white heather ;
For you fear I'm too "advanced"
To remember all that chanced
In the old days, when we danced,
   Walked, and rode together.

Trust me, Fred, beneath the curls
Of the most "advanced" of girls,
Many a foolish fancy whirls,
   Bidding Fact defiance,
And the simplest village maid
Needs not to be much afraid
Of her sister, sage and staid,
   Bachelor of Science.

Ah! while yet our hope was new
Guardians thought 'twould never do
That Sir Frederick's heir should woo
    Little Amy Merton :
So the budding joy they snatched
From our hearts, so meetly matched—
You to Oxford they despatched,
    Me they sent to Girton.

Were the vows all writ in dust?
No—you're one-and-twenty—just—
And you write—" We will, we must
    Now, at once, be married !"
Nay, you plan the wedding trip !
Softly, sir ! there's many a slip
Ere the goblet to the lip
    Finally is carried.

Oh, the wicked tales I hear !
Not that you at Ruskin jeer,
Nor that at Carlyle you sneer,
    With his growls dyspeptic :
But that, having read in vain
Huxley, Tyndall, Clifford, Bain,
All the scientific train—
    You're a hardened sceptic !

Things with fin, and claw, and hoof
Join to give us perfect proof
That our being's warp and woof
   We from near and far win ;
Yet your flippant doubts you vaunt,
And—to please a maiden aunt—
You've been heard to say you can't
   Pin your faith to Darwin !

Then you jest, because Laplace
Said this Earth was nought but gas
Till the vast rotating mass
   Denser grew and denser :
Something worse they whisper too,
But I'm sure it *can't* be true—
For they tell me, Fred, that you
   Scoff at Herbert Spencer !

Write—or telegraph—or call !
Come yourself and tell me all :
No fond hope shall me enthrall,
   No regret shall sway me :
Yet—until the worst is said,
Till I know your faith is dead,
I remain, dear doubting Fred,
   Your believing
             Amy.

NATURAL SELECTION.

1 HAD found out a gift for my fair,
   I had found where the cave-men were laid :
Skull, femur, and pelvis were there,
   And spears, that of silex they made.

But he ne'er could be true, she averred,
   Who would dig up an ancestor's grave—
And I loved her the more when I heard
   Such filial regard for the Cave.

My shelves, they are furnished with stones
   All sorted and labelled with care,
And a splendid collection of bones,
   Each one of them ancient and rare ;

One would think she might like to retire
   To my study—she calls it a " hole !"
Not a fossil I heard her admire,
   But I begged it, or borrowed, or stole.

But there comes an idealess lad,
  With a strut, and a stare, and a smirk ;
And I watch, scientific though sad,
  The Law of Selection at work.

Of Science he hasn't a trace,
  He seeks not the How and the Why,
But he sings with an amateur's grace,
  And he dances much better than I.

And we know the more dandified males
  By dance and by song win their wives—
'Tis a law that with *Aves* prevails,
  And even in *Homo* survives.

Shall I rage as they whirl in the valse ?
  Shall I sneer as they carol and coo ?
Ah no ! for since Chloe is false,
  I'm certain that Darwin is true !

SOLOMON REDIVIVUS, 1886.

WHAT am I ?   Ah, you know it,
　　I am the modern Sage,
Seer, savant, merchant, poet—
　　I am, in brief, the Age.

Look not upon my glory
　　Of gold and sandal-wood,
But sit and hear a story
　　From Darwin and from Buddh.

Count not my Indian treasures,
　　All wrought in curious shapes,
My labours and my pleasures,
　　My peacocks and my apes :

For when you ask me riddles,
　　And when I answer each,
Until my fifes and fiddles
　　Burst in and drown our speech,

Oh then your soul astonished
   Must surely faint and fail,
Unless, by me admonished,
   You hear our wondrous tale.

We were a soft Amœba
   In ages past and gone,
Ere you were Queen of Sheba,
   And I King Solomon.

Unorganed, undivided,
   We lived in happy sloth,
And all that you did I did,
   One dinner nourished both :

Till you incurred the odium
   Of fission and divorce—
A severed pseudopodium
   You strayed your lonely course.

When next we met together
   Our cycles to fulfil,
Each was a bag of leather,
   With stomach and with gill.

But our Ascidian morals
    Recalled that old mischance,
And we avoided quarrels
    By separate maintenance.

Long ages passed—our wishes
    Were fetterless and free,
For we were jolly fishes,
    A-swimming in the sea.

We roamed by groves of coral,
    We watched the youngsters play—
The memory and the moral
    Had vanished quite away.

Next, each became a reptile,
    With fangs to sting and slay ;
No wiser ever crept, I'll
    Assert, deny who may.

But now, disdaining trammels
    Of scale and limbless coil,
Through every grade of mammals
    We passed with upward toil.

Till, anthropoid and wary
  Appeared the parent ape,
And soon we grew less hairy,
  And soon began to drape.

So, from that soft Amœba,
  In ages past and gone,
You've grown the Queen of Sheba,
  And I King Solomon.

SONNETS.

HELOISE.

I.

BRIDE.

COME in my dreams, belovèd ! though thou seem
   Less kind, less noble, than by truthful day ;
   Even in sleep my heart has strength to say—
" His love is changeless—this is but a dream :"
Yet rather come at sunrise, with the beam
   Of thought renewed ; and still, when eve is grey,
   Inspire me, at I tread my lonely way,
With thine own dauntless will and hope supreme.

Ah, let me die, ere meaner moods have power
   To dim these glories that within me shine !
Give me black night or this unclouded sun,
Swift death or life immortal, in that hour
   When all my soul is filled and fired with thine,
When thou and I are equal, being one.

II.

NUN.

This is the doom I must henceforth fulfil :
   To hide my heart through days, and months, and years ;
   To look in anxious eyes, and lull their fears ;
To lose all hope, and strive with joyless will ;
To sing and pray, scarce knowing good from ill ;
   To hear stale converse, as an idiot hears ;
   To tread the cloistered courts with burning tears,
Forced backward to their fount, yet rising still.

Nay, there is comfort !   E'en the sick may smile,
   Knowing for pain a swift and gentle cure :
I can be patient, and can wait awhile,
Nor curse the heedless heavens with moaning breath :
   Though for a night my weeping may endure,
Joy comes with morn—that joy whose name is Death.

III.

ABBESS.

Sweet is life's crown of quiet ; sweet is age,
  With tranquil days, unmarred by joy or dole,
  Void of desire, save that with just control
I may administer Christ's heritage :
Long since he heard my vow, the heartless gage
  Not spurning ; took my tear-stained, love-writ scroll,
  And words of strength and healing for the soul
Wrote with his own heart's blood across the page.

Passion is all forgotten, pain is fled :
  Yet oft, 'mid idle phantoms of the mind,
    Returns my earlier Self, with scornful eyes,
    Saying—"Thou deemest age hath made thee wise,
  And knowest not that thou art deaf, and blind,
And palsied.   Live in peace ; for I am dead."

HERCULES.

This fruitage from the far Hesperides
　　I bring to great Eurystheus, feared and hated,
　　Whom I, his slave, nor hate nor fear ; my fated,
My full reward, he has no power to seize,
Nor is it bought with golden gauds like these ;
　　I seek supreme delights, untold, undated ;
　　Of joys wherewith these kings of men are sated
Right little recks the Jove-born Hercules.

I live content to bear my destined burden,
To toil unthanked, unhonoured, void of guerdon,
　　To work a tyrant's will through lonely years ;
That, neither shunning pain nor scorning pleasure,
My strenuous soul may win Olympian leisure,
　　And dwell in peace among the Gods, my peers.

PROMETHEUS AND PANDORA.

THESE pangs I bear through lingering centuries
    For slavish Man, in pity and in scorn ;
    Glad, while by birds of Jove my breast is torn
Till sunset, that I spurned his luring prize :
Yet when she came, that queen with jacinth eyes
    August yet changeful, like the sea at morn,
    I could have triumphed that mine Earth had borne
A creature fashioned in such glorious wise.

Nay ! but my will were firm, though Heaven should give
    A Goddess pure.   One only gift I seek,
Freedom for Man ; or, this renounced, I live
Self-sentenced to mine own immortal hate :
    Better the rock, the chain, the eagle's beak,
And this fulfilment of my chosen fate.

THE NEBULAR THEORY.

This is the genesis of Heaven and Earth.
  In the beginning was a formless mist
  Of atoms isolate, void of life ; none wist
Aught of its neighbour atom, nor any mirth,
Nor woe, save its own vibrant pang of dearth ;
  Until a cosmic motion breathed and hissed
  And blazed through the black silence ; atoms kissed,
Clinging and clustering, with fierce throbs of birth,
And raptures of keen torment, such as stings
    Demons who wed in Tophet ; the night swarmed
    With ringèd fiery clouds, in glowing gyres
Rotating : æons passed : the encircling rings
    Split into satellites ; the central fires
Froze into suns ; and thus the world was formed.

THE PESSIMIST'S VISION.

I DREAMED, and saw a modern Hell, more dread
   Than Dante's pageant ; not with gloom and glare,
   But all new forms of madness and despair
Filled it with complex tortures, some Earth-bred,
Some born in Hell : eternally full-fed
   Ghosts of all foul disease-germs thronged the air :
   And as with trembling feet I entered there,
A Demon barred the way, and mocking said—

" Through our dim vales and gulfs thou need'st not rove ;
   From thine own Earth and from its happiest lot
     Thy lust for pain may draw full nourishment,
   With poignant spice of passion ; knowest thou not
Fiends wed for hate as mortals wed for love,
     Yet find not much more anguish ?   Be content."

THE GIFT.

From Paradise there came, one Maytide morn,
    An Almoner of love, with gifts divine :
    To some he brought rich draughts of magic wine ;
To some, who laboured in their fields forlorn,
Sweet showers and sunbeams for the springing corn :
    Then me he called, with gracious word and sign,
    But when I looked what bounty should be mine,
One fire-bright drop he gave me, as in scorn.

" Angel ! to these thou givest present mirth,
    To those, the promise of a golden crop
In Autumn ; was my hope so little worth ?"
Smiling, the Angel answered—" Share and prove
    Their joy, if so thou wilt—in that one drop
Thou hast the life and quintessence of Love."

ANDREW MARVELL'S "DEFINITION OF LOVE."

> " My love is of a birth as rare
>   As 'tis for object strange and high ;
>   It was begotten of Despair
>   Upon Impossibility."

LOVE sought me—not the blind god infantine,
   But Love with lucent eyes and pensive brow ;
   And as I mused with what adoring vow
I should accost that visitant divine,
He said, " Think but a thought and I am thine,
   Exalting thee to heavenly heights, which thou
   Without me canst not reach ; yet ponder now,
Nor rashly to my power thy life resign ;

For never will I grant thy full desire,
   But will transpierce thy heart with many a wound,
      And in the end will leave thee sorrowing."
   Then said I—" Though thy voice be sternly tuned,
Though still thou feed, and ne'er assuage, my fire,
      Yet I rejoice, and take thee for my King."

POET AND BOTANIST.

Fair are the bells of this bright-flowering weed ;
  Nectar and pollen treasuries, where grope
  Innocent thieves ; the Poet lets them ope
And bloom, and wither, leaving fruit and seed
To ripen ; but the Botanist will speed
  To win the secret of the blossom's hope,
  And with his cruel knife and microscope
Reveal the embryo life, too early freed.

Yet the mild Poet can be ruthless too,
  Crushing the tender leaves to work a spell
    Of love or fame ; the record of the bud
  He will not seek, but only bids it tell
His thoughts, and render up its deepest hue
    To tinge his verse as with his own heart's blood.

SCIENCE AND PHILOSOPHY.

WE went a-begging for a nobler creed,
  We craved the living bread and wine of thought,
  That Eucharist which is not sold or bought,
But freely given ; yet, did any heed,
'Twas but to offer pence, or bid us feed
  From empty sacramental vessels, wrought
  Of gold or brass ; we spent our prayers for nought,
Faint and athirst with spiritual need.

Then some brought grapes, and some brought corn and
        yeast,
  Plenteous and good ; yet still we murmured, "Give !
    This is scant fare when thirst and hunger cry :
Teach us to change our garner to a feast,
  Preparing food by which the mind may live,
    Perennial loaves, and flagons never dry."

THE DOUBLE RAINBOW.

I saw the passions and desires of Man
   Blent in a thousand-coloured arc of light,
   A double rainbow; but so jewel-bright
The scarf of Iris had been pale and wan
Beside it: not the torrent-bows that span
   A river-fall at noon; nor birds whose flight
   Gleams ruby and gold; nor columned chrysolite
In caves enchanted; nought, since light began,

Could match its glories: but the inner arch
   With Joy and Anguish too intensely burned
For eyes that love the cloudy robes of March
And April, and calm Autumn's golden dress:
   Half-blinded, to the outer bow they turned,
Soft with remembered Grief and Happiness.

RECOMPENSE.

The wine-flushed monarch slept—but in his ear
   An angel breathed—" Repent ; or choose the flame
   Quenchless."   In dread he woke, but not in shame,
Deep musing—" Sin I love, yet Hell I fear."
Wherefore he left his feasts, and minions dear,
   And justly ruled, and died a saint in name.
   But when his hasting spirit heavenward came
A stern Voice cried—" Oh Soul ! what dost thou here ?"

" Love I forswore, and wine, and kept my vow
To live a just and joyless life, and now
   I crave reward."   The Voice came like a knell—
" Fool ! dost thou hope to find again thy mirth,
And those foul joys thou didst renounce on earth ?
   Yea, enter in !   My Heaven shall be thy Hell !"

TRANSLATIONS.

IDEALS.

From the German of Schiller.

Ah faithless ! canst thou thus desert me,
  With all fair thoughts and fancies gay,
With all thy joys, with all thy sorrows
  Wilt thou unpitying haste away ?
Ah youthful prime of golden joyance,
  Can nought delay thee, fleeting fast ?
In vain ! The river seeks the ocean,
  Eternity engulphs the Past.

Quenched are the suns whose gladsome lustre
  Athwart the road of youth was cast,
And banished all the fair Ideals
  That fired the rapt enthusiast ;
Dead is the faith in sweet illusions,
  Beings that in my dream had birth,
And reft away their god-like beauty
  By rude realities of Earth.

As once, with ardent supplication,
　　Pygmalion clasped the sculptured form,
Until the pale cold cheeks of marble
　　Flushed with emotion, bright and warm ;
So I, aflame with youthful passion,
　　Dead Nature to my bosom pressed,
Till she to breathe, to glow, to tremble,
　　Began upon my poet-breast ;

Till, kindling to my fiery impulse,
　　At last the Dumb her silence broke,
With answering love returned my kisses,
　　And understood my heart that spoke :
The tree, the flower, for me had voices,
　　For me the silver fount could sing :
I felt my life's re-echoing music
　　Give soul to every senseless thing.

A universe of mighty yearning
　　Throbbed in my bosom's narrow bound,
To issue forth, to live incarnate,
　　In deed and word, in form and sound :
How great this world, how nobly fashioned,
　　While yet the bud contained it all !
How few, alas ! the opened blossoms,
　　And even these, how weak and small !

Oh how, on wings of dauntless courage,
  All blissful in his dream of truth,
Nor yet by any care embridled,
  Forth on Life's journey sprang the youth !
His soaring aspirations bore him
  Even to Ether's palest star ;
For Hope, with strong untiring pinions,
  Was nought too high and nought too far.

How lightly was he carried onward !
  What power could stay his glad advance ?
How swift before Life's rolling chariot
  His airy escort seemed to dance !
For there was Love, with sweetest promise,
  And there, with star-set crown, was Fame,
And Fortune with her golden chaplet,
  And Truth all robed in sunlight came.

But ah ! those bright companions vanished
  Ere half the destined course was run,
They turned away their faithless footsteps,
  Till all had left me, one by one.
Away fled Fortune, nimbly speeding,
  The thirst to Know was unallayed,
And meeting round Truth's sunbright image,
  The storms of Doubt thick darkness made.

I saw Fame's crown, of old so sacred,
  Profaned upon a vulgar head ;
Too soon, alas, the short spring over,
  The beauteous time of Love had fled ;
And every hour the silence deepened,
  And lonelier grew the rugged way,
Till even Hope could scarcely lighten
  Its shadows by one pallid ray.

But which of all that frolic escort
  Cheered with her constant love my road—
Stays with me still, consoles, and follows—
  Yes, even to the dark abode ?
Thou, gentle tender hand of Friendship,
  Who all my sorest wounds hast bound,
With loving aid Life's burdens bearing,
  Thou, whom I early sought and found,

And thou, who journeyest with her gladly,
  Like her canst quell the spirit's storms ;
Diligent Work, who wearies never,
  Nor ruins, slowly though she forms ;
Who in Eternity's vast fabric
  But grain of sand on sand-grain rears,
Yet from the debt-roll of the ages
  Can strike out minutes, days, and years.

FRAGMENTS FROM FAUST.

I.

MEPHISTOPHELES ON LOGIC. *(Part I.)*

Meph. Be careful of your time, so swiftly flies it,
But Order teaches how to utilise it.
And first, by my advice, dear friend,
Collegium logicum attend.
For there your mind is drilled and graced,
In Spanish boots 'tis tightly laced,
That now, with warier step, it may
Go plodding on in Thought's highway,
And not, mayhap, with zigzag light,
Go will-o'-the-wisping left and right,
And there they'll teach you, many a day,
That what you once did free and gay,
At *one* stroke, easy as eating and drinking,
Needs One ! Two ! Three !—the right way of thinking.
In the manufactory of Thought,
Like a weaver's masterpiece 'tis wrought,

Where *one* jerk moves a thousand threads,
The shuttles go shooting over and under,
The threads flow unseen, entwined and asunder,
One stroke a thousand filaments weds.
Then the Philosopher, in comes he,
And clearly proves, so *must* it be ;
The First was so, the Second so,
Therefore the Third and Fourth were so ;
And had the First and Second not been,
The Third and Fourth you ne'er had seen.
The students on all sides call him clever,
But not a student becomes a weaver.
To know and describe a living whole
One first of all drives out the soul,
Handles the parts and loses none,
Save, alas ! the soul that made them one.
Encheiresin naturæ, Chemistry calls it,
Mocks itself, and knows not what befalls it.

   Student. I don't seem quite to comprehend.

   Meph. 'Twill all go better soon, my friend,
When you can qualify and quantify,
And properly can classify.

   Student. I feel so stupid after all you've said,
As though a mill-wheel went round in my head.

II.

THE BACCALAUREUS. *(Part II.)*

I TELL you this is Youth's supreme vocation !
Before me was no World—'tis my creation :
"Twas I who raised the Sun from out the sea ;
The Moon began her changeful course with me ;
Day decked herself in dazzling robes to meet me ;
Earth budded forth with leaves and flowers to greet me ;
I gave the signal on that primal night
When all the host of heaven burst forth in light.
Who but myself saves man from the dominion
Of dogmas cramping, crushing, Philistinian ?
So, free and gay, my spirit's voice I heed,
And follow where the inner light may lead,
Still hasting onward with a gladsome mind,
The Bright before me, and the Dark behind.

THE EYE.

From the German of Emil Rittershaus.

The human soul—a world in little ;
   The world—a greater human soul ;
The eye of man—a radiant mirror,
   That clear and true reflects the whole.

And, as in every eye thou meetest
   The mirrored image is thine own,
Each mortal sees his soul reflected,
   In all the world himself alone !

ON THE WATER.

From the German of Emmanuel Geibel.

Now hill and dale begin to bloom anew,
The tree-tops bud, and winds pass whispering through ;
Faint grow the bugle-notes, with sunset's red—
I would be merry, but my heart is dead.

My comrades ply their oars, and scorn delay,
The furrowed wave gleams back the starlight ray ;
To the guitar the dancing boat is sped—
Fain were I merry, but my heart is dead.

The moon is up, and clearer shine the skies,
From every bosom songs of mirth arise ;
In all our goblets wine glows darkly red—
Fain were I merry, but my heart is dead.

And could my Love rise up from out the grave,
And grant all dear delights that once she gave,
And say all tender words that once she said—
In vain !   The Past is past, the Dead are dead.

DANTE AND NINO.

From the Italian of Dante ("Purgatorio," Canto VIII., v. 43-84).

AGAIN Sordello spoke—" Into this dell,
Among the mighty Dead, now let us go ;
The sight of thee will please the spirits well.
In but three steps, meseems, I was below,
And gazing on me only, one came nigh,
Attent, as though my face he fain would know.
It was the time when eve englooms the sky,
Yet not so dusk but that a closer view
Made clear the darkling path from eye to eye.
Noble Judge Nino, how I gloried when
I saw thou wast not with the damnèd crew !
All words of courteous greeting spake we ; then
He asked—" How long since camest thou to us
Beneath this mount, o'er seas beyond our ken ?"
" I came by those dread regions dolorous
This morning, with my first life undecayed,
In hope to gain the second, journeying thus."
And when they heard this answer that I made,
He and Sordello shrank back, as in fear,

Like folk by sudden wonder all dismayed.
This turned toward Virgil—that, to one who near
Was sitting, cried—" Up, Conrad, from thy place ;
What God in mercy wills, come and see and hear !"
Then to me turning—" By that special grace
Granted to thee by Him, who from our sense
Conceals his primal Why, which none may trace—
When thou shalt pass beyond the seas, far hence,
Say to my little Joan, she must implore
For me, where heed is given to innocence.
Her mother loves me, so I think, no more,
Since she has cast aside the fillet white,
Which, heart-sick, she shall wish that still she wore.
From her thou mayest understand aright
How long will burn the fire of woman's love
Not kindled fresh by daily touch and sight.
Less nobly will her funeral pageant move
Beneath the Milan warrior's viper-shield
Than were Gallura's cock emblazed above."
Such words he uttered, seeming stamped and sealed
With that just ardour, whose attempered heat
His heart still cherished, and his face revealed.

FRAGMENTS.

WINTER AND SPRING.

To her Grandfather on his Birthday.

Oh sweet is light that dawns from gloom,
  And hope that springs from grief ;
Soon bud the violets on the tomb
  Of Winter's despot chief.

With many a death-presaging cry,
  Loud wails the hoary king ;
With clouds he fortifies the sky
  Against the warrior Spring.

But though his helmet's plume is bright
  With rain instead of dew,
With sunbeam sword the youthful knight
  Shall cleave his passage through.

But long ere he, with victor shout,
  The crown of earth shall win ;
While grim old Winter rules without,
  Our Spring sits throned within.

z

In vain the winds, with stormy strife,
   His first pale buds destroy,
If, nourished by our dearest life,
   Still blossom Love and Joy.

For though the days are darkly sad,
   And though the nights are drear,
Yet loving hearts may still be glad
   Through all the changing year.

And even Winter on the land
   A few fair gifts bestows,
Like treasures that a tyrant's hand
   Amid his courtiers throws.

In gardens that deserted lie
   Some flowers may linger yet,
And often, in a stormy sky,
   A few faint stars are set.

And so before the blossoms bright
   Have decked the earth again,
Before the jewelled arch of light
   Shines through the summer rain,

Some days will come that lift awhile
  Their veils of gloom and mist,
And, with a calm, rejoicing smile,
  By pensive sunlight kissed.

This day is fair, though stern and cold
  Its pallid brow may be ;
Where others only frowns behold
  There yet are smiles for me.

Though all the dreary land is shorn
  Of beauty, bloom, and grace,
How can I choose but love the morn
  That first beheld thy face ?

THE PRIEST'S WARNING.*

Dost long for sunrise?—quench the vain desire,
And bar thy window 'gainst the eastern fire.
Thy fathers dwelt content in sacred night ;
Walking by faith, they scorned unholy sight :
Then, reckless gazer, close in shame thine eyes,
And hide thy head, while morn illumes the skies :
Wrapped in Egyptian gloom the truth receive,
Lest haply thou shouldst see—and disbelieve.
The shapes of night, with outlines faint and blurred ;
The sounds of night, in soft confusion heard ;
The scents of night, that come from flowers unknown—
Were they not sweet, and were they not thine own ?
And he who could not rest might see the stars
And moonlight beaming through his prison bars ;
Yet blest is he who sleeps, for morning takes
These tender glories from the eye that wakes :
Yes, he who sleeps is blest ; in holy dreams,

* Originally appeared in *The Agnostic*, February, 1885.

Through day and night he sees the same fair beams.
Come, dream again ; or, if thy lawless mind
Have seen the sun, and can no more be blind,
For eyes profane as thine the daylight keep,
Nor wake the sainted souls who yet can sleep.
Yon murderer, cheered with sacramental wine,
Has higher hopes and holier thoughts than thine.
'Tis merciful to hang him, for perhaps
His convalescent conscience might relapse :
Shall new-purged eyes behold that loathsome cot,
That hideous home, where love and health are not ?
Shall hands new-cleansed caress that cowering wife ?
(Poor wretch, who knows not yet the loftier life !
Blighted and scarred, grown dull of heart and eye,
Mother of starveling children, born to die.)
What if the fiend, with seven more vile, returned,
And banished all the truth, so quickly learned ?
Yet has he passed the mystic second birth,
Prepared for heaven, though quite unfit for earth.
Straight from the gallows shall his spirit fly
To join the white-robed company on high,
Despatched in mercy to the heavenly shore,
To kick his wife, to kill his friends, no more.
But *thou*, though pure thy deeds, though kind thy heart,
In God's free grace canst have nor lot nor part ;
Thou, by unhallowed thirst for truth consumed,
With thieves, and cheats, and liars shalt be doomed :

Thy foes thou pardonest ; but thy heavenly Sire
Tortures his own with everlasting fire.
Just Ruler ! when we strive the truth to win
A false conclusion is a damning sin :
If unto thee a crooked pathway leans,
That glorious end may sanctify the means ;
But, if the straightest path should from thee tend,
The means can never sanctify the end.
Presumptuous man ! be humbled in the dust !
We are the Church of God, and he is just.
Cling to the Cross, renounce thy fruitless search ;
Better be deaf and blind than leave the Church.
Pluck out thine eyes, lest they should see too clear :
And lest thine ears mislead thee, cease to hear.
Better, a sightless cripple, save thy soul,
Than enter fires of hell, though sound and whole.
Prove sacred things by faith, if proof they need :
But prove not those which war against our creed :
Or, if thou follow Reason's polar star,
Turn back in time, nor follow it too far.
From many a distant, night-encircled tomb
Comes forth an ancient voice, a sound of doom.
The thorn-crowned ages cry : " Return, return,
In haunts of death the way of life to learn.
Ah, wherefore pine and struggle to be free ?
For what has liberty to do with thee ?
Thy fathers wore their fetters to the grave ;

Then why shouldst thou disdain to be a slave ?
Round every limb they wreathed the golden chain,
And what thou deemest loss they counted gain.
Wilt thou be free ? then Christ is not thy Lord :
Wilt thou be true ? let Hell be thy reward !"

NIGHT AND MORNING.

Night.

I LIFT to Heaven my longing eyes,
  Knowing that yonder tranquil moon
Is bright for you in Spanish skies ;
  And has she power your soul to tune,
    In subtlest harmony divine,
    With all the passionate thoughts of mine ?

No, rather let her give you rest,
  To sleep in peace, with joy to wake ;
  Yet if a dream the slumber break,
Dream of my youthful soul and breast,
  Hungered, alone, far off, and sad ;
  But dream them near, and dream them glad.

Morning.

The morning radiance floods my room,
  Its tender glow my brow has kissed,

And scattered all the night-born gloom :
   Yon floating, thin, translucent mist,
Pierced through and through with living gold,
   Makes lovelier what it half enshrouds :
And you in distant skies behold
   The self-same sun, but other clouds.
Trim English lowlands bloom for me ;
   For you Alhambra's courts are bright ;
For both o'er earth, and sky, and sea,
   Through thought and passion, mind and heart,
Still streams the same all glorious light ;
   Earth's barriers keep us far apart,
But we are one at heaven's height.

PRIZE WINNERS OF THE

CONSTANCE NADEN ANNUAL GOLD MEDAL,

INSTITUTED BY DR. LEWINS.

1890.—F. D. CHATTAWAY, B.Sc., Trinity College, Cambridge. Poem : " Persephone : A Myth Re-set."

1891.—In this year no essay was deemed worthy the medal.

1892.—MISS JESSIE CHARLES, B.Sc., Essay : "Evolution in Relation to Ethics."

1893.—MISS JANE E. PEMBERTON, Essay : " The Comparison of Dante's ' Divina Commedia,' Milton's ' Paradise Lost,' and Klopstock's ' Messias.'"

PRINTED BY WATTS & CO.,
17, JOHNSON'S COURT, FLEET STREET,
LONDON, E.C.

SOME PERSONAL AND PRESS OPINIONS

ON THE

WORKS OF CONSTANCE NADEN.

PERSONAL OPINIONS.

THE Misses Emily and Edith Hughes have received many gratifying letters in acknowledgment of presentation copies of *Selections from the Philosophical and Poetical Works of Constance Naden* (fcap. 8vo, pp. i.–xxxii., 1–190; cloth, gilt, with portrait of Miss Naden; Bickers; 3s. 6d.), among which the following are noteworthy :—

GENERAL SIR HENRY F. PONSONBY, G.C.B., writes from Windsor Castle : " I am commanded by the Queen to thank you for the copy of 'Selections from the Writings of Constance Naden' which you have had the kindness to present to Her Majesty."

COUNT SECKENDORFF writes from Windsor Castle : "Count Seckendorff presents his compliments to the Misses Hughes, and begs leave to say that he has been commanded by Her Majesty the Empress Frederick to thank them for the copy of a book, 'Selections from the Philosophical and Poetical Works of Constance Naden,' which Her Majesty has been graciously pleased to accept."

MRS. JOSEPH CHAMBERLAIN writes from Highbury : " I have received the book of 'Selections from the Writings of Constance Naden' with much pleasure, and desire to thank you most warmly for it. I shall read it with much interest, for I remember my pleasant meeting with Miss Naden, and I shall be glad to know more of what she was."

MR. HERBERT SPENCER writes from 64, Avenue Road, Regent's Park, London, N.W. : " I am obliged to you for the copy received this morning of your 'Selections from Miss Naden's Works.' They are well worth preserving, and in their present form will, I should think, meet with considerable acceptance."

DR. SAMUEL SMILES, author of "Self-Help," "Lives of the Engineers," etc., writes from 8, Pembroke Gardens, Kensington, to Dr. Lewins: "I am exceedingly obliged to you for the 'Selections from the Works of Miss Constance C. W. Naden,' sent to me yesterday by Messrs. Bickers & Son, publishers. The 'Selections' are full of profound truth, and the appended poems are exceedingly interesting. The volume will afford me much pleasure and profit during the approaching winter season."

PROFESSOR LAPWORTH, LL.D., F.R.S., writes from the Mason College, Birmingham : "Please allow me to thank you most gratefully and sincerely for the present of your most interesting and beautiful 'Selections from the Works of Constance C. W. Naden.' It is a pleasure to look at and an education to read. I have enjoyed myself this afternoon going through it, and reading again some of our dear friend's words, so thoughtful, so far-seeing, so true, and so beautifully expressed. I am sure that the book will be deeply valued by those who knew and loved Miss Naden, and will do good to those who did not. I think that you have selected and arranged your material and your subjects very nicely indeed, so that the excerpts almost read like a continuous story or argument."

PROFESSOR TILDEN, D.Sc., F.R.S., writes from the Mason College, Birmingham : "I cannot allow a single day to pass without returning my most grateful thanks for your charming little volume. I am not quite sure that I am prepared to argue that Constance Naden's *forte* was not poetry, but philosophy. Had she lived, I think we should have seen surprising developments in both directions. As it is, we who knew her feel nothing but thankfulness for what she has left us. I hope your volume will have the large circulation it deserves."

DR. T. F. CHAVASSE writes from Edgbaston : "It is very kind of you to send me the very artistic little volume containing selections from the late Miss Naden's books. It will be difficult to say whether I value more the kindly feelings which prompted the authors to present me with their book, or the intrinsic value of the spirit of the book itself. But I nevertheless do thank you very much, and, at the same time, congratulate you on the gratifying results of your energy and research. I hope the book will have a large sale."

Mr. Hughes has received many gratifying letters in acknowledgment of presentation copies of *Constance Naden : A Memoir* (fcap. 8vo, pp. i.–xxi., 1–91 ; cloth, gilt, with portrait of Miss Naden ; Bickers ; 2s. 6d.), among which the following are noteworthy :—

General Sir Henry F. Ponsonby, G.C.B., writes from Osborne : " I have had much pleasure in laying before the Queen the copy of your work, ' Constance Naden : A Memoir,' of which I had already heard an interesting account. Her Majesty was graciously pleased to accept the volume, and commands me to thank you for your kindness in having presented her with this book."

Lord Reay writes : " I have had the privilege of receiving your Memoir of Miss Naden. I am very much obliged. Though only having had the pleasure of seeing her for a few hours, I mourn the premature death of this singularly gifted lady as warmly as any of her friends."

The Right Hon. W. E. Gladstone, M.P., writes : " I thank you very much for the Memoir of Miss Naden. Everything relating to her is to me matter of deep and touching interest."

Mr. Sydney Lee, the present, and Mr. Leslie Stephen, the late, editor of the " National Dictionary of Biography," report that the latter eminent writer and thinker is preparing the monograph of Miss Naden for that monumental work.

The Right Hon. J. Chamberlain, M.P., writes : " I am much obliged to you for the copy of the Life of Miss Naden, which I shall read with interest."

Sir Philip Magnus writes : " I am indeed much obliged to you for sending me the Memoir of Constance Naden...... In common with everyone else who knew her, I was deeply shocked when I heard the sad news of her death, which so abruptly terminated an acquaintance which I had hoped would ripen into friendship."

In acknowledging the receipt of a copy of the Memoir sent to him by Mrs. Charles Daniell, MR. GLADSTONE writes as follows : "I read through the whole Memoir with undiminished interest. There can be no doubt that by the death of Miss Naden the world has lost a person of gifts both extraordinary and highly diversified. As yet I believe in her mainly for her poetry ; but a mind highly scientific is shown by the wonderfully clever verses on ' Solomon Redivivus.'   I am glad to be under the impression that we have not got the last of her remains. I shall always regret my personal loss in not having known her personally."

Finally, as a contrast to Mr. Gladstone and others above quoted, it may be noted that MESSRS. MACMILLAN, through their managing partner or director, Mr. Craig, peremptorily declined, in an interview with her literary executor, Dr. Lewins, to have anything to do with the publications of Miss Naden, even on their own terms.

The REV. E. COBHAM BREWER, LL.D., author of " Dictionary of Phrase and Fable," etc., writes :—

" MISS CONSTANCE C. W. NADEN AS AN ORIGINAL THINKER.

"One cannot hope often to have so attractive a theme as Miss Naden to write about—so fair, so young, so fresh, so talented, so full of brilliant promise ; but, alas ! it must be added, so frail and short-lived, cut off in the very bud of womanhood. The end is sad, but the beautiful little star has left a trail of light behind, and has been so happy as to have a Dr. Lewins for her *præcordium et dulce detus.* Miss Naden had the gift to see the hidden genius of her mentor, and Dr. Lewins to discern the flower shut up in *la jeune fille dans le bouton de son age.*

"It is not often that such a combination of talent as poetry and philosophy is met with in the same person ; but Miss Naden was a poet born, and made herself wise in science and philosophy. Her penetration was quick and keen, and she seems to have been about the only one able to grasp the difficult subject of Hylo-Idealism. She saw at once that objects, till they became subjects, cannot enter into the sphere of our consciousness, and therefore are to us virtually as good as non-existent.

"Many have read about Hylo-Idealism, but have been surely puzzled to reconcile it with their foregone conceptions ; but, then, every new phase of progress has this stumbling block as a rock of offence. Geology had a long uphill fight with prejudice, so had astronomy, so indeed had machinery ; but Miss Naden, from the very first, grasped the whole subject, and tried, not without notable success, to popularise what, to her own mind, was completely self-evident.

"Others of her philosophical and scientific excursions show the same intuitive penetration, and probably, had her life been spared, her name would have been bracketed with that of Mrs. Somerville ; as it is, H. Spencer says that Miss Naden and George Eliot, the two female Warwickshire poets and thinkers, are on a par, and he does not know where to find a third.

" Miss Naden's poetry has the true ring of precious metal; but, like Kirk White, Keats, and Shelley, her age was only a little, little day. But I am not going to dwell here on this subject, for another paper, by Nellie C. Hayman, entitled ' Miss Naden as a Poet,' will be found in this collection."

NELLIE C. HAYMAN, *née* BREWER, Vicarage, Edwinstowe, Newark, Notts, writes :—

" MISS NADEN AS A POET.

"In a certain choice corner of a cosy room is a bookshelf, where many favourite books are to be found. Among some well-worn and well-marked volumes, the eye is attracted by a little blue-covered book, evidently a special favourite ; it falls open easily in the hand, and various marks on the margin show that it has been ' read, marked, learnt, and inwardly digested.' The very name conjures up visions of spring blossoms, and, as the pages open, a breath of spring seems to sweep across the quiet room.

"' Songs and Sonnets of Springtime,' by Constance C. W. Naden, is written on the cover. The poems are gems: they range from grave to gay, now and then a deeper note is struck ; the song falls into a plaintive, minor key, and the sweet singer touches on the mysteries of life and death. Here is a song of ' Twilight,' in which, in the palms of ' the radiant colours in the West,' is seen 'the mystery of night,' and the thoughts lead on to the deeper mysteries of the human soul :—

> 'As height and depth alike transcend our vision,
> The human soul, whence clearest lustre beams,
> Has yet its Hades and its fields Elysian,
> Revealed alone in symbols and in dreams.'

"In the 'Pilgrim' (page 39) is a fine attempt to depict the genesis, by Dr. Lewins, of Hylo-Idealism, or Auto-Morphism (Selfism). In 'Six Years Old' the heart of a child is laid bare. The precocious child, alone in the garden, weaving her dainty fancies about the fairies, 'with thorns for their knives and their forks,' and their ball-rooms of 'white lily cups,' and that wonderful country of light, far over the seas and the mountains, which she visits in her dreams. The Sonnets speak of Nature in all her aspects, from the first snowdrop, 'Fair sunny-hearted child of many tears;' the—

> 'Lanes and woods array
> With hawthorn that was wont to bloom in May
> White petalled, crimson-anthered ;'

on through the 'barren splendours of July,' the glow of autumn, when 'the leaves flame gold and scarlet,' the dim and silent skies of November to December, when the earth—

> 'Lies dreaming of her destined hour,
> All white and still, most like a soul at rest.'

If you are in a gay mood, and want a hearty laugh, read 'The Lady Doctor,' that—

> 'Spinster gaunt and grey,
> Whose aspect stern might well dismay
> A bombardier stout-hearted !'

although there is a touch of pathos, too, in the hint of her early life, when, in the bloom of girlhood, she wandered in the dewy meadows with her young lover. She rejects love, and chooses instead the charm of powder, pill, and lotion. Nay, her very glance

> 'Might cast a spell
> Transmuting sherry and Moselle
> To chill and acrid potions.'

There is a fine touch of sarcasm in the poem called 'The

Two Artists '—one being the painter who despairs of ever matching on his pallette the pure damask rose of his mistress's cheek ; the other being the mistress herself, who knows too well the secret of the pretty bloom contained in a certain little bottle.

" The translations from the German are all very beautiful, the sentiment and spirit of the originals being wonderfully preserved. In these days of careless and slipshod translations it is a great treat to read some of the songs of the great German poets in perfect and flowing English.

" That Miss Naden herself was a German scholar is evident in her poem, ' Das Ideal,' and in the short dedication, ' Meinem Verehhrten Freunde Herrn Dr. Lewins in Dankbarkeit Gewidmet '—we know she was a true friend.

" We close the dainty book, feeling that, for a short time, we have been in touch with a noble woman, a woman whose influence would make one ' purer, better, stronger '—one ' who, being dead, yet speaketh.'

" The book is laid aside, the hands are folded idly in the lap, and, as the twilight gathers in that quiet corner, certain words of Miss Naden's own linger and echo in the deepening gloom as one's thoughts dwell on her peaceful grave.

> ' Look in her face, and lose thy dread of dying ;
>   Weep not, that rest will come, that toil will cease ;
>   Is it not well, to lie as she is lying,
>   In utter silence, and in perfect peace ?' "

MISS GINGELL, compiler of the "Aphorisms" of Mr. Herbert Spencer, writes : "The thought that has dominated my mind in reading Miss Naden's poems is that they are the expression of a mind eminently scientific, both naturally and by education, illustrating emphatically the truth that Mr. Herbert Spencer so strongly insists on in his work on ' Education,' where, in combating the general idea that science is not conducive to poetic thought, he says : ' It is not true that the cultivation of science is necessarily unfriendly to the exercise of imagination and the love of the beautiful. On the contrary, science opens up realms of poetry where, to the unscientific, all is a blank.'"

LADY BURTON, née ARUNDELL, widow and executrix of the late Sir Richard Burton, K.C.B., writes : "I have a regretful and pleasing remembrance of a tall, soft, fair girl, who, perhaps, would not have attracted much attention from a society of butterflies; but the more the Thinker looked at her, the more he felt drawn to know something about her. She was born to great things, but her brain was too big for her frail frame, and she died in Mayfair from illness contracted in India (as one might say) little more than a child, leaving the world a flower the less. She had made her mark in poetry and in science; and, if that bud had lived to open, one cannot foresee what track of light she was capable of leaving behind. She was not only a poet, but a chemist, a psychologist, and—may I say, alas!—a Freethinker. If she has left behind many admirers, she has left one faithful friend, who will always keep her memory green; and no one is fitter to sympathise with and to understand this pious work than I."

PROFESSOR F. MAX MÜLLER writes from 7, Norham Gardens, Oxford : "I am glad to hear of the appreciation of Miss Naden's poetry. I liked the poems when they first came out; but I never trust my judgment as to English poetry. I am no judge of English poetry, so far as the jingle of rhyme and the glamour of words are concerned. Tennyson once told me that the only excuse for rhyme was that it helped the memory. That may have been so in ancient times; but is it so now? My only test of poetry is: Does it stand translation into prose? It struck me when I read Miss Naden's poems that several of them would stand that test, and I am glad to hear that the world has found it out."

C. LLOYD MORGAN, Dean of University College, Bristol, writes : "Although I am not prepared to accept all her conclusions, I yield to no one in my sincere admiration of Miss Constance Naden's genius. She was gifted with rare philosophical insight, and a clearness of perception and presentation which illuminates all she has written. Combining the woman's delicate intuition with the more masculine power of firm logic, she gave promise of taking a position in speculative philosophy to which no woman and very few men have attained. And then death came just when her rich nature was beginning to mature its fruit."

MISS JANE HUME CLAPPERTON, authoress of " Scientific Meliorism," etc., writes : " It is with mingled feelings that I pen a tribute to the memory of Constance Naden. Gratified pride in that she belonged to my own sex springs up when

I contemplate her varied gifts and keenly intellectual powers; but when the moral aspects of her personality are remembered, every other sentiment gives way to poignant regret. The earnest truth-seeking of her nature and her simple allegiance to truth, when she had found it, are rare characteristics in either sex ; and there presses on me the conviction that with the too early cessation of this valuable life there was lost to the cause of progress a social force of admirable quality and widely effective range."

CHARLES LOCKHART ROBERTSON, M.D. (Cantab), F.R.C.P., Lord Chancellor's Visitor in Lunacy, writes : " I knew Miss Constance Naden very well, and I need not say that I greatly valued the friendship which she extended to my wife and to myself. I read with much interest the first volume of poetry which she published in 1880, ' Songs and Sonnets of Springtime.' I still think it full of girlish grace. In the ' Songs and Sonnets of Springtime ' I would name ' The Abbot ' as full of promise. Again, when her youth is remembered, and that her studies were all made in England, her translations from the German seem to me of great merit. Thus the Sonnet, ' Bury the Dead Thou Lovest,' from the German of Karl Siebel, is most gracefully rendered ; and I think her translation of Schiller's ' Knight of Toggenburg,' ' Life and the Ideal,' etc., may be compared with those of more distinguished translators. Her wonderful mastery of the German language is shown in the Sonnet, ' Das Ideal.' Her skill in design and taste in art are shown in the floral decoration on the cover of the volumes in question."

J. J. AUBERTIN, translator of Camoens' " Lusiads," Commendador of the literary Order of Portugal, " Saõ Thiago," and the same of the " Rosa " in Brazil, writes to Dr. Lewins : "Miss Naden's too early death was a blow to our literature, both scientific and poetical. Her pen had already achieved much for so young an author, and gave abundant promise for a great deal more. As that ' more ' has become impossible, it only remains to give every form to what she has left, and I hail your now intended publication on that ground."

SHADWORTH H. HODGSON, President of the Aristotelian Society, writes to Dr. Lewins : " The enclosed transcription of the passage in the Aristotelian Society's Committee's

Report, adopted by a General Meeting, in which Miss Naden's lamented death is recorded, does justice, as it seems to me, to the favourable impression made on the Society by her great abilities :—

"'*Extract from the Report of the Committee of the Aristotelian Society for the Eleventh Session, 1889-1890, adopted at the General Meeting of the Society, June 16th, 1890.*

"'CONSTANCE C. W. NADEN was the daughter of Mr. Thomas Naden, of Birmingham, and was educated at the Mason College, Birmingham, where she distinguished herself particularly in Logic and Philosophy.* Miss Naden was elected a member of our Society in 1888, and at once attracted attention by her clear and striking contributions to our discussions. It was her intention to have read a paper during this Session on "Rationalist and Empiricist Ethics," but her fatal illness prevented her from accomplishing it. The notes prepared by Miss Naden for this paper are printed on page 77 of this journal, as well as others which were found among her papers, on "The Place of Mental Physiology in Philosophy." Miss Naden's lamented death in December last, at the early age of thirty-one, has been the subject of very general regret, and the public press has given a full account of her life and work. The essay on "Induction and Deduction," written while Miss Naden was at Mason College, has recently been published, together with other papers and a biographical notice, by her friend, Dr. Lewins. By her death the Society loses one of its most valuable members.'—From 'The Proceedings of the Aristotelian Society,' vol. i., no. iii., part 2, page 160 (Williams & Norgate, 1890). Communicated by Shadworth H. Hodgson, President."

H. WILDON CARR, the Hon. Secretary of the Aristotelian Society, writes to Dr. Lewins : "I am glad to hear that a new edition of Miss Naden's poems is being published. I had the pleasure of meeting her often at the Aristotelian Society during the short time of her membership. She took very great interest in our discussions, and was preparing a paper for us at the time of her last illness. Her early death was felt very deeply by all of us."

* See her "Memoir" by the Treasurer of the Birmingham Corporation, Mr. Hughes, F.L.S.—*R. L.*

OPINIONS OF THE PRESS

On *Selections from the Philosophical and Poetical Works of Constance C. W. Naden.* Compiled by EMILY and EDITH HUGHES. With an Introduction by GEORGE M. MCCRIE. (Bickers ; 3s. 6d.)

———

" An elegant little book to look upon, and will doubtless prove admirably attractive to admirers of Miss Naden's philosophical writings."—*Saturday Review.*

" The volume of 'Selections from the Philosophical and Poetical Works of Miss Constance C. W. Naden,' compiled by the Misses Emily and Edith Hughes, and published by Messrs. Bickers & Son, is one of the daintiest that we have seen for some time. The selections from her essay on 'Induction and Deduction' contain some remarkably fine expressions, and many other parts of the book are of great interest."—*Nature.*

" There are, probably, a large number of persons who are unacquainted with anything of Constance Naden's writings, and to such the volume before us—a dainty little volume, gilt-edged, and tastefully bound—will give some insight into her style of work and thought. Miss Naden, who died in 1889, was a philosopher of somewhat advanced views ; we are told in the very brief introduction to these 'Selections' that 'the thought currents of our day are even now setting in the direction she indicated,' that Herbert Spencer thought her endowed with the exceptional combination of 'receptivity and originality' in an equally great degree, and that she was an exponent of 'Synthetic Monism.' Anyone who wishes to verify these assertions may do so by help of the extracts from her 'Essays' and 'Reliques' here collected."—*St. James's Gazette.*

" Miss Naden wrote charming and humorous light verses. ......We should like a complete edition of her poems."—*Pall Mall Gazette.*

" Her cult has the merit of much originality, and we feel sure that a perusal of the extracts contained in this small volume will induce a reader to appreciate it, and wish to study it in its unabridged form."—*Public Opinion.*

"The Misses Emily and Edith Hughes supply 'Selections from the Philosophical and Poetical Works of Constance C. W. Naden,' whose premature loss is so deeply lamented. The trend of Miss Naden's mind was distinctly philosophical, and her ripest energies were directed in this channel. These isolated gems shine with delightful lustre apart from their settings. It is a book which will find many devotees among the new thinkers of the day."—*British Medical Journal.*

"This volume should succeed in introducing the work of a subtle thinker to many people to whom, hitherto, the name of Constance Naden has been unknown."—*Publishers' Circular.*

"The volume is illustrated by a portrait of Miss Naden, and is dedicated to Dr. Lewins, her friend and mentor. The prose extracts precede the poetic, but the latter are more likely to attract the ordinary reader, as they abound in quiet humour. We are glad to find that charming little *jeu d'esprit,* 'Solomon Redivivus,' has not been omitted."—*Literary World.*

"These extracts show that Miss Naden had some gift for epigram, and could present her philosophic views in a clear and striking manner."—*Guardian.*

"To those who have not the good fortune to own acquaintance with Miss Naden's published writings, this selection may be cordially recommended. The passages from her philosophical essays and tracts, and the examples of her poetic genius, which are contained in this beautiful product of the printer's art, will, we feel confident, lead many readers to a study of the works themselves."—*Liberty Review.*

"Miss Naden was one of those great intelligences that, flashing meteor-like across the firmament of the world of philosophic thought, left, in her brief passage, few (yet distinct and valuable) traces of the operations of her mind."—*Bookseller.*

"Miss Naden was, no doubt, an exceedingly clever woman of decidedly advanced views on most subjects."—*Notes and Queries.*

"This is a book which is interesting and full of suggestion......Her verse, especially her lighter verse, is decidedly attractive......Her ardent character and single-minded devotion to science are more attractive still."—*Woman.*

"These selections will be valued by those who have recognised her rare genius, alike in her philosophical writings and her poems......The name of Constance Naden is probably known to but a comparative few, for the general reader takes little interest in works such as she wrote. As, since her death, however, there have been many controversies regarding her opinions, some misunderstandings and misconceptions, this present selection should help to make her writings more widely appreciated."—*Court Circular.*

"This book gives a representative series of saws, paragraphs, and poems from the writings of the gifted propagandist of Hylo-Idealism, and will be welcome to many ......who are curious about the ideas and teaching of this strange transcendentalist."—*Scotsman.*

"Altogether the book is an interesting one......and we may at least allow that the author of 'A Modern Apostle' had, in her composition, some of the true gold of poetry." —*Manchester Guardian.*

"This is an exceedingly pretty little volume......These extracts from Miss Naden's poems bring out the simplicity, tenderness, and playful humour of a noble nature."— *Birmingham Daily Post.*

"Messrs. Bickers & Son have issued a tasteful volume in the familiar covers bearing the Bell flower, containing selections from the works of the late Miss Constance Naden. The Constance Naden literature is steadily increasing...... and therefore it is that these selections, carefully, skilfully, and intelligibly compiled by Miss Emily and Miss Edith Hughes, will be of real service and high value alike to the casual reader and to the student. It is most appropriate that this pleasing and necessary work should have been undertaken by these hands......So deftly has the work been done that we scarcely notice the absence of the links, and it is possible from the fragments to obtain a true percep-

tion of the leading points in the theory of Induction and
Deduction, and its association with Evolution......The
Misses Hughes are to be congratulated upon having ex-
tracted the real ore, the essentials, from Miss Naden's
writings ; and, without being too sparing on the one hand,
or too prodigal on the other, have included what is best
and what is most just to that lady's memory."—*Birmingham Daily Gazette.*

"Admirers of the gifted young lady who was prema-
turely cut off by death some three years ago, before she
had had time to give more than an indication of her rare
talents, will welcome this elegant and tasteful little volume."
—*Glasgow Herald.*

"The object of the compilers has been to attract readers
to Miss Naden's writings themselves ; and, from the very
careful manner in which the selections have been
made, we should think that the student will be so much
interested in the extracts as to desire to peruse the books
from which they have been culled."—*Midland Counties
Express.*

"The personality of the late Miss Naden is familiar to
most Birmingham people who are interested in literary
matters, and probably few are unacquainted with the striking
series of philosophical essays by which she showed most
conclusively that it is possible for a woman to grapple
successfully with some of the deepest problems which
present themselves to thoughtful minds. The present little
volume, choice and attractive in its external aspect, is a
loving attempt to bring together, in a moderate compass, some
of her most pregnant observations, together with a selection
from her poems. Miss Naden's vigorous and determined
search for truth, her strong and clear exposition of her
theory of ' Hylo-Idealism,' and her lighter and more playful
side, as shown in many of her poems, are all well displayed ;
and no reader can fail to be attracted by so interesting a
catena of thoughts from so powerful a mind. An excellent
portrait of Miss Naden is prefixed to the book."—*The
Central Literary Magazine.*

"Miss Naden's works are well known to our readers, and

their merits are so universally recognised that it is unnecessary to say one single word in praise of them. It was a happy thought which induced the Misses Hughes to prepare this charming book of selections. They are derived from all Miss Naden's published works, her two volumes of poems and her prose works issued since her much deplored death. The extracts have been selected with great skill and discrimination, and they will do much to make a wider circle of readers acquainted with the philosophic insight, power of giving lucid expression to abstruse thoughts, and the literary excellences of the greatest local genius of modern times. The book is well printed and handsomely bound."
—*The Midland Naturalist.*

"We notice with much interest a volume of 'Selections from the Works of Constance C. W. Naden,' compiled by Emily and Edith Hughes, with an introduction by George M. McCrie. It is always a pleasure to meet with fresh indications of the far-reaching influence of Miss Naden's philosophical and literary works, and the present volume is likely to be especially useful in interesting those who are not already acquainted with her books. The selections have been made with much care and thought, and are calculated to give a considerable insight into her philosophical teaching. About two-thirds of the volume is devoted to extracts from the philosophical writings, the remainder to the poems. Among the latter we note the exquisite 'Pantheist's Song of Immortality,' probably the best known of her poetical works, and also the charmingly humorous 'Scientific Wooing,' 'The New Orthodoxy,' and 'Solomon Redivivus,' the first of which appeared in the *Mason College Magazine*, when Miss Naden was one of its leading spirits. The volume is well got up, and in every way suitable for a gift-book. We wish it every success."—*The Mason College Magazine.*

"The chief difficulty that meets the critic is that of selection amid the wealth of intellectual matter to be found between the covers of this beautiful little tome......The ladies are to be congratulated on the excellent way in which their task has been accomplished ; not least in choosing for the outside decoration of the book—and a most beautiful one it is—the favourite flower of the dead authoress, whose work and memory they have done so much to immortalise."*—*Rochester and Chatham News.*

"This chaste little volume is the result of much earnest research through the writings of one of the most remarkable women of modern times. Miss Naden, whose premature decease was recorded about four years ago, was a native of Birmingham, and her wonderful intellect enabled her to grasp the most difficult of scientific and philosophic studies. ......We advise those of our readers who are unacquainted with the writings of this talented lady to acquire the anthology which the Misses Hughes have so diligently prepared."—*Herts Illustrated Review.*

——————

[After these authoritative eulogies the only censure I can find is contained in an insignificant print, *Sylvia's Journal,*† which is answered by me in the article here reproduced, entitled "Constance Naden and Materialism," in which the criticaster's ignorance and presumption are fairly exposed.—R. L.]

"One would like to speak only in the kindest way of this selection from the work of an interesting young writer, who died a year or two ago ; but, notwithstanding Mr. Gladstone's praise of her, the fact cannot be disguised that a very great deal has been made out of a very little. The work, which is published by Messrs. Bickers & Son, of Leicester Square, is beautifully produced ; and, if the editing had been on a par with the publishing, Miss Naden's memory would have been better served. The two ladies, Miss Emily and Miss Edith Hughes, whose names appear on the title-page as the compilers, have evidently done their labour of love with care ; but they appear sadly lacking in literary judgment in regard to the selection. Many extracts are given which are utterly unworthy of being served up as single gems ; for, so far from being tersely, epigrammatically, or happily expressed, they strike one as inexpressibly commonplace and obvious.

————————

* *Notes by Dr. Lewins.*—The selection is by Miss Naden herself, and is to be found in her two earlier poetical volumes ("Songs and Sonnets of Springtime" and "The Modern Apostle," etc.).

† I do not mention one or two scurrilous articles in the *National Observer,* a journal conducted on Jingo and "Patriotic" (see Dr. Johnson's definition of the term) lines, as the scurrility is directed, not against Miss Naden, whom it designates Titania, as against her Executor, vilified as "Bottom."

Opening the book at random, the first gem I light on is: 'Before reprobating *(sic)* any statement as false, we should take care to inquire into the facts, that truth may ever remain inviolate,' which is only another way of saying that two and two make four. On the next page I open I find the following startling statement standing by itself: 'The name of Plato is the greatest in Greek philosophy,' which is scarcely less likely to be denied than the incompetency of Miss Naden's editors. But for pretentious and utter gratuitousness commend me to the introduction, which is, we are informed, by Mr. George M. McCrie, who is apparently more anxious to 'introduce' Mr. George M McCrie than Miss Naden. The book is a lamentable example of the old adage, 'Preserve us from our friends.' "

**

CONSTANCE NADEN AND MATERIALISM.

To the Editor of " Sylvia's Journal."

SIR,—Perhaps I may be allowed, as literary executor of the late Miss Naden, to make a brief comment on your somewhat depreciating notice of her poetry and philosophy, which have extorted the approval of thinkers like Herbert Spencer, Dr. Samuel Smiles, Dr. R. W. Dale, Lord Reay Mr. Gladstone, and other notabilities.*

The difficulty in the way of a satisfactory appreciation of her thesis is well cleared up by her own essay, "What is Religion?" and by my pamphlet, "Humanism *v.* Theism," and also by Mr. G. M. McCrie's leaflet, "Sadducee *v.* Pharisee" (Bickers and Son). Its gist may be summarised in a very few words by characterising it as the *subjectivation of the objective*, exactly Kant's negation of "Thing in Itself," the high-water mark of that cosmopolitan metaphysician, a standpoint from which he receded in all his profound works after the *first* edition of the "Critique of Pure Reason." It is nothing new, but only the present high-water mark and position of contemporary exact science and ethics. It is clear that, on these *selfist* data, each individual sentient being *creates* and determines its own cosmos and entire existence

Sixty years ago Wöhler succeeded in transforming inor-

---

* See *Sylvia's Journal* for January, 1894, page 101.

ganic compounds into the organic *Urea*. Now, this proves, beyond the possibility of rational dispute and doubt, that no hard-and-fast partition separates these seemingly distinct natural kingdoms—the organic and inorganic—from each other. Life, therefore *(biogenesis)*, is no novel innovation, but simply a more complex arrangement and modification of *not-life*, all forms of which are fundamentally abiogenic. The conventional notion, immemorially held as a sacrosanct tenet, that a special Divine element enters into human vital phenomena, is thus seen to be an illusion having no ground in reality. This *scientific* substantiation is, in our time, the great *desideratum*, not merely the *great Perhaps*. —I am, Sir, yours, etc., R. LEWINS, M.D., *Surgeon Lieut.-Colonel (R.).*

Army and Navy Club, Pall Mall.

OPINIONS OF THE PRESS

On *Constance Naden: A Memoir*. By WILLIAM R. HUGHES, F.L.S., with an Introduction by PROFESSOR LAPWORTH, LL.D., F.R.S., and additions by PROFESSOR TILDEN, D.Sc., F.R.S., and ROBERT LEWINS, M.D., Surgeon Lieutenant-Colonel (R.). (Bickers ; 2s. 6d.)

"To Mr. Hughes, who is responsible for the greater portion of its contents, much gratitude is due from all friends and admirers of Miss Naden for the great and loving care which he has devoted to the task of writing a faithful and sympathetic sketch of her short but brilliant career."—*The Literary World*.

"This volume, which depicts in sympathetic style the life of the gifted lady whose name forms the title, is a work of love that Mr. Hughes has given to the world of her admirers, which were very numerous, especially in the Midland capital. Her philosophic turn of mind, her thirst for scientific knowledge, and her keen appreciation of art marked her out as a prominent character in the history, not only of Birmingham, but of science and art. Mr. Hughes has prepared a Memoir which shows great care and does him great credit."—*The Metropolitan*.

" It is a marvellous record for a woman who died when she was barely thirty."— *Woman.*

" The strength of the impressions made by the late Constance Naden on her friends is now further declared by the little volume of Memoirs put together by three or four of them......They serve perhaps better than any one sketch could do to tell how remarkable were Miss Naden's abilities, how deep was the sense of loss that fell at her death on all who knew her, and how lovable and estimable was the moral nature with which her rare mental powers were bound up."— *The National Reformer.*

" Her intellectual development is a great testimony to the value of modern scientific education, and her Memoir should be studied by all who are interested in the training of what is often unfairly stigmatised as ' precocious ' intelligence."— *Manchester Examiner.*

" Miss Naden, who died on Christmas Eve, 1889, at the early age of thirty-one, was a devoted disciple of Mr. Herbert Spencer,* and, during her short but brilliant career, has written many essays on scientific subjects, which indicated such a remarkably keen intellect as to call forth admiration and comment from her most distinguished contemporaries.   Mr. Hughes's pleasantly-written Memoir is appropriately supplemented by contributions from other personal friends—viz., Professor Lapworth, LL.D., F.R.S., Professor Tilden, D.Sc., F.R.S., and Dr. Robert Lewins, of the Army Medical Department."— *Herts Advertiser and St. Alban's Times.*

" Miss Naden was a lady of undoubted genius, not only as a poetess, but in the more abstruse paths of philosophy ; and her early death, at the age of thirty-one years, is a national loss......Mr. Hughes is a loving as well as talented chronicler of Miss Naden's life, and his scholarly attainments are well seen in the Memoir."— *Chatham and Rochester Times.*

---

* *Note by Surgeon Lieut.-Colonel Dr. Lewins.*—Miss Naden's admiration for Mr. Spencer was undoubtedly very great.   But her own originality was such that she cannot properly be termed his " disciple." The Royal Society's motto, *"Nullius in Verba,"* etc . was, with her, quite instinctive.

"The book is altogether one that will assist to a perfect conception of the marvellous character which developed so mightily, and shines out with so intense a radiance—a radiance which our eyes, unused to such, must be prepared for to understand aright."—*The Birmingham Daily Gazette*.

"The Appendix to Mr. Hughes's Memoir of the late Miss Constance Naden—that remarkable poet and student of science whom Mr. Gladstone's well-remembered reference helped to make famous—comprises a letter from Mr. Herbert Spencer, who pays a high tribute to the powers of his young disciple :* 'I can think of no woman [he says], save George Eliot, in whom there has been this union of high philosophical capacity with extensive acquisition. Unquestionably, her subtle intelligence would have done much in furtherance of rational thought, and her death has entailed a serious loss.'"—*The Daily News*.

"Gifted beyond the ordinary lot of woman......An enthusiast for art, and a writer of poetry of no mean order, the real bent of her mind was towards the study of philosophy."—*The Publishers' Circular*.

"Excellently done, in a simple and telling style."—*The Mason College Magazine*.

"She died too soon.   She achieved much ; she promised more ; had she lived twenty years longer, I believe she would have taken a great and enduring place in English literature."—DR. DALE, in *The Contemporary Review*.

"It is, indeed, a valuable tribute, not only to the remarkable intellectual powers of the subject of the Memoir, but to the value of the educational means we possess, and by which those powers were fostered.   Mr. Hughes's little book is well written, well edited, and well printed."—*The Midland Institute Magazine*.

"We have only praise to give Mr. Hughes for the admirable manner in which he has dealt with the very miscellaneous materials placed at his disposal, and for the generous appreciation which has enabled him to do justice to all sides

---

* See footnote on previous page.

of an exceptionally rich and complex character."—*The Central Literary Magazine.*

"......The book is printed in clear type, paragraphed, and easy to read. It is full of the most instructive and interesting matter which it is possible to put into print—namely, the ardent, unceasing struggles of a human soul during its whole life upon earth to know something of its environment, to understand the why and the wherefore of all things. The story fascinates as it is read, and it is not difficult to perceive that a kind pen, a wise pen, the pen of one who knew Miss Naden well, has written these pages......"—*Shafts.*

* * * *

" This little work ('Induction and Deduction') acquires a melancholy interest from the fact that the talented young authoress has not lived to see its publication. The title essay, on 'Induction and Deduction,' gained in 1887 the Heslop Memorial Medal, provided out of the proceeds of a bequest to the Mason Science College of Birmingham by the late Dr. Heslop, and awarded annually by the Council of the College.* It is clear, concise, well arranged, and carefully thought out ; and leads one to believe that, had the hand of Death been withheld, Miss Naden would have made valuable contributions to philosophic thought. For Miss Naden the fundamental principle in philosophy is the famous Protagorean formula of relativity, that 'man is, to man, the measure of all things, of things that are that they are, and of things that are not that they are not.'† She insists on the close inter-connection of induction and deduction in all reasoning, the two processes not being antagonistic, but complementary. Both involve cognition and recognition ; but, whereas induction is a process of cognition involving recognitions, deduction is a process of recognition involving cognitions. The historical development is traced from the Greek cosmologists, through Plato, Aristotle, Bacon, Descartes, and Locke, Mill, Jevons, and T. H. Green; and

---

* It may be mentioned that a marble companion bust to that of Dr. Heslop, of Miss Naden, has been placed in the Library of Mason Science College.

† This formula of the more sober Berkeley of antiquity is quite misrepresented by Plato when he objects that, if so, it must be the same in the case of the Baboon. No doubt it is so to that " poor relation."—*R. L.*

there are many signs that Miss Naden had not merely grasped, but assimilated, the teachings of those whose influence on the theory of reasoning she traced......"—PRO-FESSOR LLOYD MORGAN, Dean of Bristol University College, in *Nature.*

" Miss Naden's departure from this world has left a blank which it will be hard to fill up. England and India both have reason to mourn her loss, as she has identified herself with all great movements in England, and was also thinking of doing something in this country in remembrance of her visit to the Indian peninsula. The prominent part she took, in conjunction with Dr. Garrett Anderson, regarding medical aid to Indian women, endears her name to this country, and entitles her to our gratitude and respect. To her personal attributes, which were so brilliant and varied, it is difficult to do justice. As a real thinker, genuine debater, and eloquent speaker, she remains almost unrivalled among her own sex, and I cannot describe with what attention and admiration her friends met at 114, Park Street, on Saturdays, which was her home day, to listen to her brilliant conversation."—U. S. MISRA, Barrister-at-Law *(Extract from the Indian " Pioneer ").*

R. LEWINS, M.D.,
Surgeon Lieut.-Colonel (R.).

Army and Navy Club, S. W.

WORKS BY THE LATE CONSTANCE NADEN.

SELECTIONS FROM THE PHILOSOPHICAL & POETI-CAL WORKS OF CONSTANCE C. W. NADEN. Compiled and Arranged by the MISSES EMILY and EDITH HUGHES, and illustrated by a Portrait of MISS NADEN. With an Introduction by GEORGE M. McCRIE, Author of " Further Reliques of Constance Naden." Cloth, 3s. 6d.

INDUCTION AND DEDUCTION. A Historical and Critical Sketch of Successive Philosophical Conceptions Respecting the Relations between Inductive and Deductive Thought; and Other Essays. Edited by R. LEWINS, M.D., Army Medical Department. With Memoir and Portrait of the Author. 1 vol., 8vo, cloth extra, 7s. 6d.

FURTHER RELIQUES OF CONSTANCE NADEN. Edited by G. M. McCRIE. 1 vol., crown 8vo, cloth, with Portrait and Autograph Letters, 7s. 6d.

A MODERN APOSTLE; The Elixir of Life; The Story of Clarice; and Other Poems. Crown 8vo, cloth, 5s.

SONGS AND SONNETS OF SPRINGTIME. Small crown 8vo, cloth, 5s.

WHAT IS RELIGION? A Plea for Individualism. Paper wrapper, 8vo, 1s., by post 1s. 1d.

BICKERS & SON, Leicester Square, W.C.

WORKS ON CONSTANCE NADEN & HYLO-IDEALISM.

CONSTANCE NADEN : A Memoir. By WILLIAM R. HUGHES, F.L.S., Treasurer of the City of Birmingham. With an Introduction by Professor LAPWORTH, LL.D., F.R.S., President of the Geological Section of the " British Association " at Edinburgh for 1892, and Additions by Professor TILDEN, D.Sc., F.R.S., and ROBERT LEWINS, M.D., Surgeon Lieut.-Colonel (R). With Portrait. 112 pp., cloth, 2s. 6d.

CONSTANCE NADEN AND HYLO-IDEALISM : A Critical Study. By E. COBHAM BREWER, LL.D., author of " Dictionary of Phrase and Fable," " The Reader's Handbook," " The Historical Note-book," etc. Annotated by R. LEWINS, M.D. Paper wrapper, 8vo, 1s., by post 1s. 1d.

SADDUCEE *versus* PHARISEE : A Vindication of Neo-Materialism. In Two Essays. I. Constance Naden : A Study in Auto-Monism. II. Pseudo-Scientific Terrorism. By G. M. McCRIE. With an Appendix reprinted from the *Journal of Mental Science.* Crown 8vo, price 6d., by post 7d.

HUMANISM *versus* THEISM ; Or, SOLIPSISM (EGOISM)= ATHEISM. In a Series of Letters to CONSTANCE NADEN by ROBERT LEWINS, M.D. Crown 8vo, wrapper, price 6d., by post 7d.

BICKERS & SON, Leicester Square, W.C.